THE GANDY DANCER

&

Other Short Stories

by

B.D. Sparhawk

OH! WHAT A LIFE I LEAD PUBLISHING COMPANY
YOSEMITE / BIG SUR / BROOKLYN

and

TRAFFORD PUBLISHING COMPANY
USA / CANADA/ UNITED KINGDOM / IRELAND

First Edition

Order this book online at www.trafford.com
or email orders@trafford.com

Most Trafford titles are also available at major online book retailers.

Printed in the United States of America.

ISBN: 978-1-4120-1874-6 (sc)

Trafford rev. 8/15/2014

www.trafford.com
North America & international
toll-free: 1 888 232 4444 (USA & Canada)
fax: 812 355 4082

THE GANDY DANCER
&
Other Short Stories

PREVIEW

Inside THE GANDY DANCER & Other Short Stories are unforgettable, timeless, very human characters, brought to riotous life by a spirited, single American woman. A buccaneer.

B.D. Sparhawk, after decades of Brooklyn, in poverty and prosperity, spanning many careers, picks up and heads west, uproariously detailed in OUTPOSTS, SIGNPOSTS, STEAMBOATS, AND THE WILD BLUE THUNDER ON THE ROAD TO MANDALAY. "The Blue Thunder," her noisy 1974 Suburban, coaxed out of a southern turnip field and a Virginia preacher, takes her, and her Labrador, and six cats across country as they flee nazis, hurricanes, and camp out in Big Sur. Torrential storms pound the Pacific coast. She's trying to write her first novel.

GRANDPA'S TICKET TO RIDE opens the book on a memory of childhood and Sparhawk's only and electrifying meeting with her once wild, red-haired grandpa, who lives up to his legend and then some.

SARAH'S JIVE: Vermont and New York in the sixties, and the complex underpinnings of the unhinged youth of America, and making choices. Sparhawk goes for the tightrope, not the net.

MIDNIGHT MANHATTAN is the story of a little runaway boy, found in New York City by the author and her four-year-old son. They treat him to "A Hundred And One Dalmatians" and popcorn; but cannot, later, soothe the desperation of a diamond hunter on a slippery slope, clearly gone bad.

RODIN OF THE BLUE RIDGE, and VANGUARDINIA are pure animal...part and parcel of B.D. Sparhawk's life. A chocolate Labrador, Rodin, found near death in the Blue Ridge Mountains of Virginia, becomes her cross-country pal.

VANGUARDINIA is the remarkable, brave kitten discovered with her family in a wilderness barn, back east.

In the course of THE GANDY DANCER & Other Short Stories, the reader is carried from Brooklyn to Biloxi, Big Sur to the Sierra Nevadas, on a road trip not matched since Kerouac.

THE GANDY DANCER, the title story, finds Sparhawk managing weddings on a fancy California horse ranch. And a gem of an old man called Pop, in the midst of his granddaughter's million dollar wedding, brings the reader back to the America of the Depression and riding the rails. Pop lays out the hard and fabulous life he led, ridin' boxcars. And "Jesus! We was free! So free!"

EDITH'S STORY recounts the journey of a woman Sparhawk meets who, on her own passionate road of discovery, learns her son has been killed. Edith reclaims her life through a miracle encounter.

All of the stories in THE GANDY DANCER & Other Short Stories are touching and surprising, O'Henry twists to Jack London yarns. This delightful, original collection, full of beautiful imagery of land and skies and people, are stories of the USA told by an American girl, raised coast to coast, and north to south, who took off on her own at 17 to see what's up. There's persistent virtue to each adventure, as it reaches heart and soul for a rare look at the lives strangers choose for themselves. The classic independent spirit of the American adventurer is captured in each short story, and the everlasting joy of charting new territory. Has anything, she asks, got more of a punch to it than a road map?

DISCLAIMER:
> These are called stories for a reason: bits and pieces of my life come together in a great bouillabaisse on these pages, and the people and events, in keeping with tradition, have had some liberties taken with reality, but most of it is bonafide, names and places changed to protect the usual suspects.

ACKNOWLEDGEMENT

How many people does it take to enrich a life? I can't count that high. There are outstanding ones, with more meaning to me than you, but if you met a single one you'd be thrilled.

Sheila G., who'll always be my best friend. Chris B., and Jim J., guiding me through previous careers and knowing this one was afoot. Dick; Dennis; and J.F., J.R., B.K., Q., and all the swell guys; L.B., and J.A.; and Rick who I'll always love. And Trevor.

The extraordinary teachers: Dr. N. Isabel Wright, who made me whole; Roberta Sari Kaplan; Caroline Higgins; Peter; Ed & Martha; Dorothea. Friends who listened to countless readings: Deborah, Rhiannon, Misia, Nina; encouragement from Jacki, Randa, Teresa, Ann; David and Nancy; Jane and Ray; Uncle Rich and Aunt Viv. Thanks, Doctors Richard H., Joni B., and Chris C. And Janet Woods, wherever you are, I'll never forget your invitation to your Maine island when we were kids. Gilda, thanks for your remarkable self in my life. And Charles, there is no other like you. And thanks one and all and to ones not mentioned here for the privilege to know you. Randy & Char, but for you Carmel Valley Market and kindness and extended credit, I'd have starved. And unending thanks to my buddy Deborah Effron, who transformed type to the marvel of computer disk, who put up with midnight edits, and who mixed praise with rebuke as only she is able to do.

I won't leave out my heroes of land & sea & air: Lewis and Clark, T. Jefferson, Charles Bronson. Longfellow & Donne, Earhart and Alex the Great and Dolly Parton, Davey Crocket and Dan Boone & Clint Eastwood, and every thrilled and thrilling pioneer adventurer. Thanks, Marie Curie and Thor Hyerdahl & Chuck Yaeger & Rand McNally. You've all done so much for me.

To Rodin

THE GANDY DANCER
&
Other Short Stories

CONTENTS

Illustrations appearing throughout THE GANDY DANCER & Other Short Stories were drawn by the author. The author took the photographs which appear in this book, except for Grandpa Alfred (photographer unknown).

Format and Transcription by Deborah Effron.

"My Lost Youth" by Henry Wadsworth Longfellow, reprinted by kind permission by MacMillan and Company.

THE GANDY DANCER
&
Other Short Stories

INTRODUCTION

When I was very young I thought life an unfolding rapture which multiplied each sunrise: a bright-lit pathway into glowing air. I still do. And find, to my surprise, life also comes with climbing hills up, dropping down the other side, then mustering for another climb and a revitalized view. Living creatures come equipped with resource, and taking risk is ours to use, not leave in idle.

I've done some travelling and even stood stock still on frenetic Brooklyn byways, sandworn Biloxi, pond-side porches of Sierra Nevada cabins, even downtown St. Petersburg / Leningrad / St. Petersburg. Adventure, the substance of life, is to be had anywhere, any time. Suddenly you're privy to something you didn't know before, and that something calls outloud to leap you in, and forward ho! Into the magic episodes of life, which do link and do connect, even glistening briefly in the midst of grueling effort. So, if you've never had a wrong day, you're not living right.

Living a life is heroic, says my pal Sheila. She's right. And there is much of it to be done, with courage and guts. You can pull that out of yourself or the very air when the need arises. In any abundant starry starry night, or rays of lilac dawn, friends and animals and geography I've loved come on the run to me and I to them to make the sad go on the slip like silt, off a dream that is good and powerful and worth paying attention to.

The book you've opened is about to touch ground on a few of my journeys and I hope their telling provides adventures different from the ones you've had.

How do you do, at long last.

I

Grandpa's Ticket to Ride

The Blue Thunder

Grandpa's Ticket To Ride

Preambling

One thing that happens when you're on the move is the need for a whole new take on who the hell you are. Locale and real estate can do much to define you if you stay put. The sound your front door makes, the sight of dandelions at pavement splits, the smell of blossoms on that tree down the block, the o'clock your neighbor gardens in her straw hat, even where your socks are…it all adds a kind of stability that goes right out the tail pipe as soon as you hit the road.

I was discombobulated by it initially. So I set up new references, like learning how to navigate by the stars. I'd never had any sense of direction, so I had to improvise. Here I am, I'd say, in relation to that tree, or that blue sky, or that crocus on the trail. Like Snoopy, here is the World War 1 Flying Ace, heading for the café and the pretty little Parisian girl. Okay, now I know where I am. I would carry my part in the world on my back. Actually, that's entirely reasonable, especially if you go from Downtown Brooklyn to Big Sur.

And then I started adding things. I guess I'd call them locators. One dish, one hat, a photograph to remind me who I was even when the landscape I knew vanished. A kind of fuzzy, happy thing going on, a kind of, hello, that's me, all right, on to the next.

But for many years, I'd pared down to near buck neked, albeit in second-hand clothes somebody else broke in, to walk scenery I didn't know. I'm with Thoreau on that, old clothes are the best. And no household around me anymore. I figured out pretty quick I'd have to do something to keep myself from dropping off the deep end. There's a metamorphosis just crossing the Rockies.

When I was camping in forests, I took side trips to a town with a snazzy home furnishings store to buy, on the installment plan, a beautiful and impractical sugar bowl with lid; a creamer; a small dessert bowl and large plate, all with a wildly extravagant

colorful pattern of gold and red pomegranates, heavily embossed, made by an English firm. So pretty. So gently spendthrift. And with all my pretty things in storage on the other side of America, these oddities perched on the car's mantlepiece or current picnic table added all the pizzazz I needed to remind me of all I was missing.

It came as a surprise that I had counted on neighbors and neighborhoods and the faces of friends, too. And once the unsettling shock wore off, I found it extraordinarily interesting, ready to explore it a bit and see just how far I could go, and what effect it would have and could I get transformed by it. I already knew I could get transformed by new experiences. I liked it. Miraculous eye-openers happen all the damn time.

Likewise, there were things to soothe, to remember my character if the usual defining forces avalanched: My paintings. My ink drawings. My writing. My animals.

Which is to say, off on the prowl for new experiences, in virtual solitude, winnowed down to a few combustibles and comestibles, and a previous life gone in the heated fume from the exhaust pipe, there's an odd, empty-handed moment that comes up. It left me wondering, wait a minute, I've disengaged from everything I used to know. Was that smart?

I mean, surely who I am is not paraphernalia. Even if I bear in mind: the house is gone, and all the stuff in cardboard boxes, nothing waiting for my return…it's waiting to be sent for! Not that it didn't place me in good company with pioneers, but it did intensify the midnight who am I rumblings.

So there I was, and all my neighbors were trees and birds. I know how I got there. I'm not some amnesiac.

❖   ❖   ❖

I rented a cabin deep and high in the Sierra Nevada wilderness. For six years, I'd moved around the country and planned now on a year in one place, nestled in Ansel Adams skies, to write a book.

3

A deceptively pretty winter night spread through the valley before me. I watched its last yellow-green light on the pond below, then came in off the porch with an armload of firewood for the woodstove. The pleasant chore accomplished, I poured myself a nice glass of Australian port, and fell into my old overstuffed armchair to watch the fire's strength. Serious weather was coming. You could feel it.

There was a modest week-old snow on the ground. The Yosemite peaks were solid white. The air had a dense quiet, hovering in wait for the energy of the storm to sweep it into havoc, that silent kind of hesitancy that can hold itself aloof and breathless for forty-eight hours, that maiden for her knight in the castle aerie, take me take me, in whispered lunacy, until the storm answers, rivets and wracks the high ebony thick wind, pulls up everything in its path to explode in blanketing blinding snow. And in these violent stratospheric dancings, pyrotechnics lash the granite mountains, the canyons roar and shake, and waterfalls flatline, frozen into blades of ice.

The weather-tested cabin would keep me warm. There was food and drink; flashlights, candles, and kerosene lamps for illuminating; propane for hot water and cooking. I had not written for three days. I had things to do. I would find out what they were eventually. The storm would help. I rubbed my hands together in anticipation.

I had a hand-crank radio to entertain. There wasn't much more to speak of inside. My art supplies and portable easel stood across the room. I had over two thousand books and one bookcase. So they were mostly stacked on the floor, sentinels to narrow passage in every direction. The desk with my typewriter, typed pages organized in piles; a pink fluted glass lampshade from the late 1800's of Paris hung from a brass fixture, swinging above it. Some wooden chairs and stools dear to my heart, two simple cotton rugs, and then my plants at all the windows, red and white geraniums among them and a peacock of an asparagus fern cascading down ten feet from a top shelf. And my large white and beautiful cat, Gorgeous, who landed on my lap and meowed to remind me of his suppertime as I inventoried my curious surroundings.

I fed him a bowl of the raw ground beef he loved and watched him devour it, his size putting lie to any want in my care. I filled a big copper pot with water and put it on the propane burner to start for spaghetti, and lit a cigarette. On the wall next to the small kitchen window, I reread the three signs I had scratched out on 8½ x 11 typing paper: Fellini, on one. Flying Buttress, on another. And Piebald, on the third. I could never say any of them enough.

I liked excess, but a wild and varied internal landscape became an expensive obsession while there was still so much new territory to chart. Tuesday I would deal with the closet. Partly because it was tomorrow, and partly because it was as good a day as any to examine suitcases, trunks, hats, the boxes of the saved and the unworn.

My friend Judy was coming to visit for the purpose of breaking up any boredom of the task at hand. She would be sensible and firm about what had to go. Also, she had just opened a second-hand store in town. We would fill her car.

I ate my pasta awash in butter and minced garlic, parsley and celery chopped fine, salt and pepper, and matched the last mouthful with the last paragraph of Ernest Shackleton's journal, "South". Intrepid explorer, quite a guy. And I'd have to re-read it to state it with certainty, but I don't think he ever wrote the word 'fear', despite the awesome weather or the fact they made camp on ice floes.

With all of civilization within my reach, in my bountiful country, I had felt fear, and did not like it. Being fearful made me angry the minute I realized that it served only to exclude me from all I sought in this universe in which I live. I did not want exclusion.

The pots and dishes left in the sink, I went up to bed. As Gorgeous and I climbed the stairs, I calculated, again, how little I needed for a good time.

Tuesday dawned. I watched its prussian progress and opal sun. Migrating ducks fluttered noisily off the pond. A dog barked from somewhere, hidden by dark and distance. I could smell the snow laying in wait above the High Sierras. I looked down the road, and it was still clear enough for a car to make it in.

5

Judy had much in each day of her life to enchant her, and she would not fail to answer every call along the way. It made her ETA uncertain. I could start the job, and maybe, because it worried me each plunge, prevent the outpiles of clothes from growing too large, filled with things I could not bear to never see again. A gray silk shirt that had some place in my past, a citron scarf. If I kept tossing one after the other, would I disappear? I would tackle sweaters first. They had come to rest on the corner back closet shelves.

In among them and about to touch my life anew, was a long forgotten robe which I had carried unfailingly with me since childhood, for reasons I will soon divulge.

Judy arrived before noon. She made me go through the pile twice again, and was ruthless but well informed.

"You don't need this," she said flatly.

"Yes I do!"

"Do you ever wear it?"

"Yes."

"When's the last time you wore it?"

"Uh, wait a minute..."

"This is not your color anyway. Stop making faces."

"But it's blue!"

"It's the wrong blue."

"I wore that, last year, or..."

Judy shot up her eyebrow and waited. I protested. I caved. She was too good at this.

We went back inside my closet, separating wearable anything from what to toss, when she pointed at a bag, pulled it out, and said,

"What's this?"

"Some artifact of my past," I said, sarcastic in my surrender. Then I recognized it. I took the carefully packaged robe from her hands.

"My God," I said softly. "It's my grandpa's ticket to ride."

I slid it from its wrapper of plastic, and pale blue tissue paper, and tried it on. Then Judy tried it on. All the memory came crashing back, right into my heart, like the first day I saw it, in a different time, on a different coast, when I was just a kid, years and years ago.

❖   ❖   ❖

The robe had come from my grandfather, whose name was Alfred. I met him only once, amid much emotional sturm und drang when I was fourteen and my family was moving from Pennsylvania to California. My mother wanted to take me with her to see him in New York City, to say hello and say goodbye. They hadn't spoken for fifteen years, prior to this arranged meeting. I was thrilled to meet my grandfather, despite the terrifying images that had been set out, which only served to make me drool, not shudder. What fourteen-year-old does not want to say hello to a reprobate relation with a pirate's past, shrouded in mystery. I kept my dark rumblings shored up. The display of emotion at home was frowned upon.

I was being properly raised in a world of white gloves and girdles and any hideous plain undergarment that would pinch short the exuberance of the living. I don't know my mother's frenzied source of this kind of control. Maybe born of poverty's dreaded spectre and having not; maybe despairing dirt from cities and their skies and streets she was raised on, of desperate clawing at the wind, just to rise above and out of the uncouth, and the unclean.

And maybe because I did not face those particular battles yet, it had not become my own mission. Though at the time, I had no clue as to what I was sinking in, or how to set myself free. I didn't like constraint, but I went along, uncomfortable but unprotesting. The scream stayed deep inside me, until I met its echo in Damon Runyon and Jack London and George Orwell, in Rudyard Kipling and Neitzche, James Agee and Fellini and Cocteau, and oh the long list. Simmering in me was a loathing for convention, and I was begun, in youthful angst, on my journey to find out why I so hated its deadening presence. I was restless.

My Grandfather Alfred gave me two presents on the only day we met. One was simply a robe, though rare and beautiful, a robe.

The other gift was my first sight of an irregular life well led. The ceremony of both took place in the last minutes of the visit to his New York City apartment, which he now shared with his second wife, who was Scot and heavily prettily brogued, whom I had been instructed to call Aunt Joan.

On rare and unexpected moments in my youth, the tiniest snippets of my grandfather's life came howling out of my mother like steam from a pressure cooker, and just as quickly vanished into silence. A missile hurtled across the room from which you had to duck, started invariably with:

"That sonovabitch! He did…" this and he did that. I never expected to meet him.

And later in my life, there was the photograph of the young dapper Alfred sent to me by my mother. She was finally resigned, I think, to whatever damage he may have caused and my great distance from its repair.

The photograph was sepia. He was spotless elegance and comfy in it, a dark suit and white shirt, a tie, a flower of modest proportion in his lapel and a handkerchief in his pocket. But it was grandpa's face that riveted the camera into which he looked with a wonderful arrogance and heat through the pale blue eyes that side of the family was famous for and were passed onto everyone but me. He was leaning against a tree, a very large cigar between his fingers, incredibly handsome and looking as if he had just finished a meal of the world and was taking time to rest before doing it all over again.

The photograph was marked with his name on the back, and in equally careful script, the year 1912. I took him to be in his middle twenties. His nickname, because of the color of his hair, was 'Red'. I'm guessing, though I only heard "Grandfather" or, in a way that made me accountable for him, 'Your Grandfather', that he was called Al, too, unless he objected. He had the ready energy and build of a fighter to him, and if he hadn't liked being called

9

one thing or another he probably scrapped and handled his fists well.

When I was growing up, the family made regular visits to my father's side of the family in New York City, until their Florida retirements and our moving away. Nonetheless, I learned very little about their lives or pasts, or dreams. That grandpa smoked a pipe, many pipes, stuffed with cherry tobacco, and played pinochle with his sister, and Mr. and Mrs. Grumbul from next door. He comforted me for things I was unaware of suffering, and I loved him.

I never met my mother's mother. But my mother's father, this stranger-father, my other grandpa, this unknown, unremarked on man remained just that through my first percolating decade and a half that led to that day.

Alfred walked the earth and had a life in which he was young and strong and dangerous. Those exploding facts that telegraphed out of his daughter and ricocheted around the room, could not be investigated in safety, and stayed bad ground to travel, painful and enraging to the messenger. He came from another country, each brief report naming it anew:

"Where did your dad come from, mom?" I took a chance.

"Denmark…he was a holy terror."

"I thought you said it was Finland."

"I don't know. A holy terror, that's enough."

"Oh! I remember now, you said Italy. Was he happy?"

"He was always pleased with himself."

"How did he get here?"

"I don't know!" She looked at me. "Stop making faces."

My mother's hand on the ironing grew more fierce, the steam rising.

"But he got here somehow." I forged ahead. "How did grandpa get here?"

"So many questions! Don't make me burn your father's shirt! Who cares how he got here! He stowed away on a cargo ship."

She said it with some exasperation, I think, at his impossible nerve.

"Wow! He did! Really? My grandfather?"

"Technically, he's your grandfather. Yes. Yes, he stowed away, twelve years old and he stowed away on a cargo ship. Really."

I thought I saw her smile. She put my father's white ironed shirt on a hanger.

"And, mom? Then he came here to America?"

"Well, he didn't get thrown overboard! They found him hiding, and they were way out to sea, so they made him a cabin boy. Two years, sailing around all over hell and gone and then he got to New York harbor and he jumped ship. And that's the truth."

"You mean, he jumped off the boat!"

"Don't be stupid." I was accustomed to the reproach. "You could try to help me out, bring that pile over here."

I hauled the washing over, but resumed my seat at a safe distance. I wanted answers. Sometimes the danger was worth it.

"You mean he jumped off the boat?" I tried it again, and had no other way to form the sentence in my mind.

"Yes, yes. He jumped ship. That's what I said."

"Wow."

Oh wow. Oh grandpa. Wow.

"Don't you give me 'wow'! That sonovabitch, he..." and so on.

❖　　　　　❖　　　　　❖

What was not to like? As if the red hair and a nickname of his own wasn't enough. I imagined him ruthless, swashbuckled, armed to the teeth, and found him, frankly, irresistible. My mother would never forgive him for his temper, for hitting her and her sister, for leaving them starving half the time when they were little. She looked okay to me now. I was a long way from examining the trauma any of that can cause. And my parents both frightened me. Maybe I just liked to hear about grandpa because he was mythic, because everything about him was so remote. It was like finding out I was related to Captain Marvel.

The big day came without preamble, and my mother was braced for the pilgrimage to meet her father, accuse him of her undoing, and never see him again. She took me along. I don't think it was because she was proud of me. It wasn't going to be a presentation of a youthful gem, and the last laugh. I was being used as a buffer, and no matter, I was ready to admire him, at the least, and worship at his feet at the most, without letting either cold-hearted intention slip out.

I was breathless on the train to New York City. And crushed that I'd been forced into a frilly pink frock and white gloves, no way to meet an incorrigible red-haired, no-account son-of-a-bitch, but I was docile in my youth, and had yet to discover that being bored (no, Peggy Lee), was not all there was. Any virtue heretofore attributed to dull complacency was about to go up in smoke this fine and dreadful day of summer and Mom couldn't do a thing about it. I was on the hunt myself for a lovely colliding with something never before spoken of in my presence: OPTIONS. Hallelujah and bring 'em on. By the time the front door of our house had closed behind us and we had crossed the street, it was too late. My own clawing at the wind had begun.

I think Grandpa Alfred lived in the Bronx, but I was a kid and not a New Yorker and had no idea. We headed to the city. I was warned, again, and it was teary hard for my mother, that the grandpa was dirt mean and hated everything and everybody. Mom was a stranger herself to me that day as we climbed steps up and down to different platforms, changing trains. She was a bundle of rawness, showing far more emotion than I'd seen in her before, sentences shortened to, "Wait here," and "Hurry up." I was hot, suffering in too many layers of clothing that had to be kept spotless, and only eager to learn how to jump ship myself.

My mother never let me in on her troubles in a real way with talk from the heart so I could feel for her. I was young enough to be upset when a parent is upset, but no, we weren't close and it stayed that way. My connection to my mother was a lot like she had with her father, more fear than solace. I couldn't talk to her any more than she could talk to him.

New York was fast and fabulous and screaming and turgid. Dirty, wild, and overstimulating. My first Disneyland, Six Flags and Palisades Amusement Park all on one island. We arrived at the front door of grandpa's apartment building, and my mother, after one more of a morning of heaving sighs, pushed it open.

It was an elevator building, which meant it had at least six stories so an elevator was the law. No fancy doorman. No pilot. You pushed the big round button on the brass plate yourself. The door rolled open with its diamond shaped window. You pushed the big round black button inside on another plate, your floor number printed on it in white. Doors shut. Machinery chugged. You prayed and looked up and down, and the thing climbed and stopped and bounced and the doors slid open. Every floor you passed on the way provided something...music or shouting, laughter, and aromas. I hope the old apartment houses of New York still contain the rich and layered smells of thousands of lives and homeland recipes, the acrid sweat of despair, and the liqueur of success, too, rubbed against and painted into their walls. It was neither fair nor foul, just teeming mortal perfumery.

We stopped at our landing. Grandpa lived here.

I don't recall my mother's white gloved knock, or the front door of Grandpa and Aunt Joan's place which I'm sure had a peephole and lots of locks, or how it opened into the inevitable hallway. But there was a bright yellow sunlit room we came to as we followed Aunt Joan, and there were raised up venetian blinds, and curtains, and a linoleum floored kitchen, and a kind of happy clean sweetness to the apartment, and a very old man in a wheelchair who turned to look at us. His back and head were straight, his torso strong. But a craggy face this holy terror had, and maybe part of a smile on him for us. The chair turned, his face and eyes gone from connection to the visitors, and certainly the man not ready for touching for I don't think there was a handshake or a cheek kiss or anything of the kind.

Who are you, who are you, raced to fill my lungs. I want to know you, I want to know you, all but leaving my mouth in words. And knew there wouldn't be time.

The time was swift indeed. My mother spoke recrimination and cried. Scots Aunt Joan was the silent stoic, tightlipped and sad, and wouldn't come between them. It must have hurt her. She loved my grandpa and you could see it. But Joan had a dignity of character in her soft ways. I think she liked my mother, too. And knew that all the words and feeling had formed years before she met her husband, and it was not her doing and not hers to undo.

13

I saw a lot in this Aunt Joan. She was twinkle and gentle flesh and warm touch. And married to grandpa thirty-five years, and how could that be, him such a villain? Maybe on this day alone, alongside the daughter, and grandchild just met, they played a false scene for us. Maybe once we'd gone, they'd skate the linoleum in their socks, or dance in jigs, or, in exotic leaps and perfect timing and scarves to the wind, would lance the draperies with their swords. I hoped they did.

That I was heartbroken that a red-haired stowaway boy could come to such an end left me quickly. He didn't move or speak in a familiar way, in a way I was used to from adults, and it intrigued me. I think he had a plaid robe on, but maybe I'm making that up. I didn't know any grownups that were not fully dressed midday. The movement of the chair was nervous, from one place to another, angry eyes averted, gestures of futility with one hand, a long arm that was freckled and graceful, long fine fingers that one day before my time had hauled sail and cargo and curled in fists to wield pain, and fight for survival in the world, in a world I had yet to meet. He didn't seem to hide his feelings or deceive, another first, an unimaginable first to me.

We all made our way awkwardly through the long minutes. Because of her nature, I'm sure Aunt Joan had set out cakes or shortbread, embarrassed me with a child's glass of milk, and definitely brewed tea, but I don't remember, or if we were any of us in shape for swallowing. Or sitting in place, facing each other. No, it was Grandpa Alfred's back, going places, down a hall, into a room and out, wheeling now I think about it, away from the penetrating glances and tears of his own daughter who he probably didn't recognize, and certainly didn't know.

At one point he said, quite loudly, to me,

"You don't have to put up with anything you don't like, little girl."

I had no idea what he meant.

Somewhere in the last minutes, I remember all of us back in the kitchen. It produced a very private heart-stopping surprise in me when Grandfather Alfred looked straight at me and me alone, to size me up, then turned on the metal wheels of the chair that held his every harbor and ship and open sea and blue sky now, and off he went to the bedroom at the end of one of the halls.

I had followed him, and I don't think I'd have had the nerve unless a bidding had come at me from him. I discovered him bent over a large, round-topped wooden sea chest at the foot of the bed, right on the other side of the door, undoing fastenings of bolts and buckles and straps and locks. He raised the lid. I stood not far behind him.

"Don't you ever buy a ticket. You find the way, work or sneak, but never put down cash for passage, you hear me?" He shook his head. "I never put down cash for passage, not once. Oh yes, wait a minute, once, but then I didn't use the ticket, got my money back! Hah!" He looked at me. "Life does not come with a ticket, you hear me?"

I nodded.

He put his hands under one knee and shifted the leg out the way to get closer to the trunk.

"Grandpa," I sad quietly, "don't your legs work?"

"They hurt," he smiled at me. "I used them up. I walked the world, after all. Used them up. I walked on land, and hell, I walked on water! I climbed and carried and pulled and stood firm. Now they hurt."

"I'm sorry," I said. Then, meaning it because it was my own experience, "Maybe they'll get better soon!"

He continued digging without notice for the neat stuff stacked in pretty piles, making a grunting dismissal. So I didn't say any more.

He turned to look at me, softly.

"There are things that don't change. Listen," he held my hand. "You take risks in your life, little girl. Take risks, and then at the end, you say you really lived! You hear me?"

His hands were warm and strong and filled with life.

I nodded.

"Do you go to the library?"

"Mom got me my card when I was six."

"Then she remembered something, after all."

"What do you mean?"

I think he kept insulting her, but if he was it was entirely a new experience to hear. Suddenly grandpa grabbed my shoulders, nearly pinched and then let go. Was he going to kill me? Was Mom right? But he rested his strong hands once more on his knees and asked me in very nearly a whisper, while my heart pounded:

"Do you know what's out there, little girl?"

"In the kitchen?" I whispered, too.

"No, no child, beyond that, out there!" He waved his arm across the sky.

"New York City?" I was, out of practice, trying to answer right.

"Beyond that!" Grandpa laughed. It was the laugh, and loud, of a happy man, not a pitiful angry one. And not laughter deriding me, not at my expense, and I, at once, realized the difference.

"Don't answer more," he said, quite gently, "because I assure you that you do not know what's out there and I suggest you go have a look. What you find, will amaze you. I guarantee to you that is the truth. You hear me?"

I nodded again, but this time something was bouncing around inside me.

He found and then brought out of the old chest a bundle he was pleased to find and I couldn't see. He placed it on his lap, dropped the sea chest's heavy lid with a bang, wheeled around to face me and thrust out a slippery, bulky pillow-like thing, wrapped in blue tissue paper which crinkled delightfully.

Grandpa looked into my face, the sizing up again, still holding out his present until I was absolutely sure he meant for me to take it. I did, and found it hard to contain for its loosey-goosey form, and nearly dropped it.

"Don't fall short, child." But it wasn't critical of me; it was something else I'd never thought about. "You look strong. Oh, nobody told you that? Your mother's strong too, but I see her now and think, she gave up somewhere. Do you know what I'm talking about?" He kneaded his hands together. "I say to you, take on what comes your way, child. And love every minute of it, hear me? I loved your mother, too, but she won't remember it. Doesn't

16

care to! She's got a hole in her where her heart ought to be. She never learned how to love, and maybe that's my fault."

He rubbed at his lips with his knuckles, then headed back down the hall. The ceremony was over. I had some electrical short-circuit thing going on in my body, all of it good. It was more like listening to stirring music than any comprehension of specific notes. Like standing next to a roller coaster, ground level, feeling the wind on your face, but not yet on the ride.

Grandpa instructed Aunt Joan to put the package in my hands into a brown shopping bag, which she did, and returned it to me. I was grateful for the hiding of it. I wasn't big on emotional display myself at the time, and could feel, very keenly, the catch to all this, the lurking danger, the sides to take.

"It's the robe, Alfred? You've given her the robe?" asked Aunt Joan.

"Yes I did. I gave the robe to my granddaughter." Grandpa looked over at his wife, and they smiled at each other. Then he pressed his hands together under his chin, and recited:

" 'I remember the black wharves and the ships,
And the sea tides tossing free,
And Spanish sailors with bearded lips,'
That's Longfellow. Know who he is?" he asked me.

" 'And the beauty and mystery of the ships,
And the magic of the sea.' It's called, *My Lost Youth*, and Longfellow wrote it."

Aunt Joan added another stanza, which they finished in unison:

" 'And the voice of that wayward song
Is singing and saying still,
'A boy's will is the wind's will,
And the thoughts of youth are long, long thoughts.'"

Then Aunt Joan said, "D'ya ken it, child?"

I said I liked it, and threw caution to the winds to recite the first few lines of "The Midnight Ride of Paul Revere."

My mother looked amazed at me.

"Very good," Grandpa said. "You know some Longfellow after all. Now then. Don't ever buy a ticket to ride. Then find a way, work or sneak, make it right later, but don't buy a ticket. I never paid for passage." Grandpa looked at my mother who was getting alarmed.

"Oh, now! Teach your granddaughter to cheat!" She looked to Joan for help. "Joan! Don't let him…"

Grandpa ignored her. He was on a roll.

My grandpa was very loud and caused a lot of ruckus, I thought.

"That," he pointed to the bag I held tightly, "I got that in China, so many years ago. We set into port. I was a boy, a girl gave it to me, a young Chinese girl, pretty, too!"

He looked up at his Joan beside him and smiled a rascal's smile, which was taken by the wife who knew him well for what it was. "I was a kid, just a kid," he said. Then, angry to my mother, "I always paid my way, in some form! That's all I said!" Then back to me, "Gulf of Siam, I think, yes by God, the Gulf of Siam! Did he write about China? No, maybe, but he knew the life, 'Black wharves and ships…beauty and mystery of the ships…' Longfellow. They teach you Longfellow in school, honey? I found him, by myself, in the library. The men on board, they taught me my letters. They taught me my numbers. Longfellow I found myself."

He called me Honey.

Grandpa nailed me with those pirate blue eyes again, and I looked right back at him. The paper sack and blue tissue paper and silk against me, my arms in a sweat against the thing, lest I commit the sacrilege of dropping this ancient relic from a misty time, when, most foreign of all thoughts, my grandpa was a kid.

"For you, honey." He said it again. "You risk anything you have for adventure, you hear me?"

"Yes, Grandpa."

"It's your life to live, yours alone. You hear me?"

"It is?"

"Sweet Jesus." Grandpa wiped his brow. "Jesus save us."

I looked at my mother.

My mother looked faint. She pulled me away, and left her hands heavily on my shoulders.

"Risk it, you hear me!" Grandpa shouted. "Goddammit, leave her be! I'm instructing the girl!"

"She's my daughter! Don't you tell her what to do! You can't yell at me! And stop cursing! Joan! Please!"

"It comes from Shanghai!"

Grandpa said it very loudly. He patted the hand Joan had rested on his shoulder.

"That's all I said, that's all. All right, all right." The color had risen fast in his face, and now only his cheeks remained brushed with the blood brought up.

"Know where Shanghai is? It is in China. Know where China is? Well, your grandpa was there, back in 1894, maybe '96, I was there all right, and back again, and more than once. Well. All right, all right."

In that last look between us, the sailor's blue eyes were watery. Aunt Joan handed him a handkerchief and got us out the door.

My mother was talking to herself all the way down in the elevator, and as she hailed us a taxi to Penn Station. She put her arm around me and asked if I was okay.

"My heart's beating really loud," I said happily.

"Take a deep breath. You see? That's my father. Oh, God!"

But I didn't think the commotion inside my body would ever go away.

Then there was little more from her, and she was off by herself, even as we sat or walked side by side.

"I shouldn't have," she said. And,

"I'm glad I did!" And,

"What the hell was I thinking!" And,

"Well, it's goodbye now for sure, you sonovabitch, isn't it! I'm going to California! Take that! He was so old, I wasn't scared."

She turned to me in the line at the ticket window, trains in rumbling vibrations on the level below. The monster's robe clutched tightly in my arms.

"You met your grandfather. Goodbye! That's it! End of story! That was my father, the holy terror!"

Tears were running down her cheeks.

19

We settled into the Pullman train car, and doors slid and banged, and the pistons on the massive steel wheels began to turn. I lay my head against the window, drifting in and out of sleep, clutching the bag tightly. My mother tried to take it from me to jam under the seat, but I wouldn't let her.

I'd lost my white gloves. A flurry of searching took place and they remained unfound. It wasn't the first time. My mind was filling with a raucous collection of images, of ships and sailors and the open ocean, of the pretty Chinese girl who gave what had now been given me, to my grandpa, The Holy Terror. They must have had a ceremony, and then he told her to take risks in her life. And the whole family was there, all of them in silken robes and drinking tea, and thanking my grandfather Alfred for pulling their pretty little Chinese daughter out of the Gulf of Siam and saving her from drowning. Then I saw a picture of the harbor at night, the Harbor of Shanghai under starlight, they fell in love, but his ship kept bellowing its warning horns and pulling away, and he ran to the end of the wharf and she'd taken off the robe and run after him to give it to him and he swore he'd never part with it. Now he'd given that job to me. It was so incredible! So sacred! It was like church! Then I saw the harbor in New York, and there was the pretty Chinese girl again, and they flew into each other's arms and kissed! I woke up like lightning had hit. My God, my mother must be Chinese! Then I'm Chinese! And it was all so wonderful.

I fell back against the corner, my head humming on the speeding train's window glass, the summer night darkening the countryside. Now it was my job to keep the silken robe safe, for in one way or another, and it was suddenly many things, it was a love letter.

When my mother and I got home, it was late at night. We'd eaten at a coffee shop downtown Pittsburgh, in silence. As we went through the front door, finally home, I couldn't contain it anymore and asked my mother if she was Chinese.

She looked at me incredulously, and felt my forehead.

"Go to bed, okay? Sleep it off, and don't remember anything he said, okay? It's over and done, and that's the ball game. And no," she said, her voice pitched high, "we are not Chinese!"

So I never asked that again, but I was sure when I was married and having my first baby, the lie would come undone.

I hadn't finished.

"I don't want to go to bed. It's my life!"

"You do what I tell you!"

"Grandpa says I don't have to put up with anything!"

She slapped me across the face. I went to bed. I didn't cry long. Something in me was growing, and I liked it.

The moving across country seemed far away from me that night. I had little concept in me of past and future and their real content, or of aging or dying, living or visiting. Or the end of the ball game. And no idea how far away California was, except I'd heard boys and girls went barefoot there without a scold. That my family, who did not pay much attention to privacy or private possessions, might take the robe from me, was a danger I feared I might not be able to avoid.

Alone in my room, surrounded by boxes, I undressed in the dark and put on my white cotton nightie and got into bed. I listened to the sounds of the house and my parents downstairs, until it all subsided and the night grew still. I pulled at my eyelids. I got up and danced on my rug. I brushed my hair. I played Indian scout in the dark, hiding from cowboys in the trees outside my window. I wiggled my toes. Anything to stay awake. When it seemed safe, I switched on the little lamp next to my bed, finally sure no one would be awake to see the signal of my midnight secrets.

I pulled the shopping bag from under the bed and onto my pillow, and sat crosslegged, facing it. Then I reached in and carefully extracted the pile of blue tissue and batted the shopping bag to the floor.

I patted the tissue flat, rearranging it, then finally, one side at a time, drew it back from its middle parting, to see what it held.

It took my breath, and that's the truth. I'd never been this close to anything so spectacular in my life. I'd seen things in

21

books and museums, and my mother had one evening dress that was green watered silk. But this was off and away something else and it belonged to me.

It was work of ancient skill. Fine black silk that moved like clouds move, and heavily embroidered on that in thick white silk thread arose fierce and sunbursting faces, one in front and one in the back. There was more broad and heavy white silk on the sleeves and the hem, in the shape of waves. The entire robe was lined in patterned blue silk, and not a stitch frayed. I held it against my cheek, for the soft beauty of it, and for the Alfred Grandfather I would remember now in days and years to come.

I stood on the bed and tried it on, and turning, looked at myself in the mirror across the room. I was blond, and already tall. It looked as if two cultures had collided in one mirror, and everything was wrong, except that it was mine. And more than that, the robe of black and white silk dragons was very strange, and the strangeness very beckoning, and I was smack dab in the middle of it.

It was a costume of considerable grandeur. A robe with no girlish princess to it, but a seriousness. I felt important.

The robe was heavier than most clothes I wore, and up until those fourteen years and beyond I'd never be famous for my wardrobe, mostly then and still a scattered wrong-fit mish-mosh. I was not an outfit kind of girl. More than that, I had certainly never worn anything which could ever have been called splendiferous, and I was in that now.

I turned left, then right, and cinched it in and drew it out barely seeing my own amazed face above it. What possessed that man to suppose this graceless child with a bad haircut and no form could carry off the wearing of a jewel?

No one would likely ever see me in it. I intended to enjoy this. I had never been in silk before. It was an emersion in a deep warm pool. I closed it over me once more, then turned off the light to shed one piece of clothing at a time, putting it on, taking it off, getting down to naked and then lay on my bed in the intense sensuality, trying to imagine the hands that had sewn it, imagine the time it had taken to make it perfect, and the thousands and thousands of miles it had traveled to reach my hands, across rolling seas, along dry carriage filled highways, the sounds it had picked up of dockside fights and barroom brawls, tucked all the while under the unassailable arm of a sailor intermittently swilling drink and punching out the foe.

And the robe, my robe, companion to a rough woolen pea coat. The world in 1894. My body was shaking. I was sure I would never be the same. I pulled the collar up around my face, my arms lost inside the sleeves, enveloped in transporting softness. I dreamed that night of everything in the universe.

I woke early the next morning and took off the silken shimmering thing, and carefully folded and wrapped it again in its blue tissue, and put it in one of the packing boxes in my room and slid it into the back of the closet, taped closed, my name written on it. This thing I had taken a ride in.

❖   ❖   ❖

I had something new to reconcile in me that came with the day's dawning. I wasn't sure how to handle it. I was thrilled, after all, with a gift from a man who had hurt my mother. She had been kind enough not to take it from me, or threaten my keeping it. And she had, for some reason, not interfered with my experience of meeting him, myself.

I was frequently told, "You solve your own problems, little girl, don't bother me for everything." And the way to get through something rough, "You just stand it."

But somehow, if I granted he'd been cruel in earlier times, he had in some marvelous way opened doors for me, which was entirely different from either parent, who always seemed to be closing doors and locking me out. Does an unfeeling son-of-a-bitch keep, admire and love elegant things? I would have to not bother, stand it, and sort it out on my own.

There were any number of times that day I ran back to my room, pulled out the box and touched the surface, just enough to hear the tissue crackle inside, then slide it back out of view. I don't want to make this up, but I think I had a terrific day. The world appeared to be a different place. For one thing, it excited me.

❖   ❖   ❖

The family moved to California. Nothing was familiar and all of it was extraordinary.

Three days after my graduation from high school I drove across country for the summer, and drove back again in the fall. I have never literally jumped ship, but two years later I jumped off a moving train in Moscow that was headed the wrong way, following my suitcase out an open caboose, armed soldiers less than fifty feet away who lifted bayoneted rifles to their cheeks, pointed at me.

I spent a year at art school in London, and later, Paris, and Moscow and Warsaw, before returning to New York. Then Vermont. Then Mexico and parts west. A life, generally speaking, up to my elbows and shoulders and neck I hope Grandpa would've approved. Sometimes falling short but mostly learning the ropes. The robe stayed with me. I've learned how to take risks and I've learned how to fight for what's important to me.

❖   ❖   ❖

Grandpa Alfred died. I don't know when, there was no announcement of it in my parent's home, and none of it sent to me elsewhere, and I missed the emotions of it.

In my memory now, he's free from the chair a sailor must have loathed, wrapped in colorful sweet re-entry to ports and adventuring. And, I hope, a grandchild was remembered, too, who he met once and gifted with a silken robe from old China, that ticket to ride he'd saved for me that one day we saw each other, never knowing we would.

❖   ❖   ❖

I still don't know who he was, but maybe I've met other men like him. I've fallen in love with dangerous interesting men, and even a sailor once, an FBI agent, undercover NYC cop, a Louisiana wildcatter, and a Himalayan mountain climber. And maybe I've looked for the spark of vitality in the faces and actions of men because of him, life in the eyes, the jut of a jaw.

The fantastical images of Grandpa Alfred are hopelessly melded with the genuine, a patchwork of real and imagined. The day I met him, he said things to me that bounced off and sank in and whirled round my head. I never could ask about him again. When my mother finished with something, that was it, end of story. I kept my opinions about him to myself.

I am so very very sorry that my Grandfather Alfred never knew that in all my life afterward, when courage deserted me, I invoked the name and red hair of the stowaway twelve year old sailor, whose spirit was planted somewhere in me, to make me strong.

There's no admission price to life, you said.

That was the real ceremony, wasn't it, Grandpa. You saw what I might become, my very soul in danger of death, and threw me the lifeline. Whatever you may have been, whatever the record of your ways may be, you helped me. If I'd been smart enough, or brave enough that day, that's what I'd have thanked you for, but I hadn't used it yet! I can say it now. Thank you, Grandpa Alfred, you Captain Marvel, you Holy Terror, you heart of my heart. I remember you all the time.

II

Sarah's Jive

Sarah's Jive

I attended, briefly, a small college in Vermont known for its independent spirit, life in the rough, co-ed dorms, and a tiny eclectic student body.

The co-ed dorm, a not so very large old Victorian farmhouse, was filled up, and I was a day late for registration. So I got, instead, the upper floor corner room in an old barn of another wood house, off the edge of the main path, and a roommate from New York whose name was Sarah.

The college emphasized open classrooms and optional attendance, no grades, no tests, wandering professors, and hoped to foster self-discipline in we, the young. If you hadn't evolved sufficiently by eighteen, you wouldn't learn anything from the classes you weren't going to. I chose not to attend, and not be accountable for anything, and I wasn't. I've changed a lot since, but at the time it looked like a plan.

Sarah, on the other hand, was a serious only child scholar, from a long line of New York Jewish scholars. She went to all the classes, and some she wasn't signed up for which she audited, and spent the rest of her time in the library. She had a wonderful wardrobe. She groomed herself thoughtfully, and especially her luxuriously gleaming mane of thick chestnut hair that fell in waves to her waist. She was petite, and she was orderly. She had immovable pride in her worth, and she was a little underhanded. In every way, we were miles apart, but for the last.

But I was impressed by Sarah. When she slept, dig this, she did so with her arms folded above, and hands clasped behind, her head. No, impressed isn't near strong enough. It flabbergasted me. How could anyone actually fall asleep in that vulnerable position? I went to bed in layers of clothes, fetal position all the way. I tried Sarah's way once, and it scared the hell out of me. Oh, man! How did she pull that off?

Sarah never liked to do anything alone with just herself for company. I was not her choice of buddy. She made and received regular phone calls to and from home. She got three letters a week, one from each parent and one from an aunt in Chicago. There was only one phone, downstairs by the front hallway. Our mail got stuck in pigeonholes on a wall outside the dining room, so we all knew that much about each other. I called my mother once and my father twice in four months. I got one letter from a high school boyfriend. He'd written I LOVE YOU in pencil and hadn't signed it. I tossed it away as juvenile.

The little school was also famous for being closed tight from mid-December through January. All the students returned home or went somewhere. Some parents showed up and rented houses and everybody slept in the floor and went skiing and found out how to tap maple trees for syrup. Land was a hundred dollars an acre in that neck of the Vermont woods. Some students got married, bought land, and built houses. And that was, like, cool as a moose.

But from September to December there were plenty of distractions. Before the cold set in, old quarries became hidden swimming holes, and great places to spend a day. There were hiking trails to mountain tops. Some of the students were making movies and everybody was an extra. Canada was north and New York was south and a day's drive would land you in either one. Music, from banjo and fiddle and guitar to church organs, was a big part of daily life. A local farmer was teaching students who helped with his chores how to build harpsichords from scratch. Painting classes in a jerrybuilt studio and operated by a mostly drunken painter in beret, were ongoing whenever you stopped by, and it was next to a great little river. The school even had a tennis court.

I was really free for the first time in my life, and it was heady stuff. I wanted to and did gobble up everything that came my way or I could find. I bought a one-time delivery truck, probably from the late thirties, with a rounded top and a good motor. It was called a Carry-All, and it did.

We had a busy drama department. I was in all the plays. I learned make-up and lighting and moulage mask and death mask making. But not a lot about acting because I didn't take direction well. Being told what to do, like, that bugged me.

Sarah studied and read and mostly I saw the back of her head in our room, and her spectacularly shining brushed hair, and a wardrobe I envied. She even had earrings to go with everything. She was the calmest, most together eighteen-year-old I'd ever met. She didn't share much of anything, not with me. I think she thought me common, and I pretty much stayed clear. She was spiteful if given the opportunity.

Sarah went home for Thanksgiving, back to New York and a big family gathering. I had one parent in California and another one in Massachusetts, and I stayed put and ate turkey leftovers with a handful of stragglers, the iconoclast crew of us decidedly pleased to be excluded from holiday events we'd suffered through since birth. Besides which, we were cool. I think we had a food fight. And then talked about what we were likely to do over Christmas and nobody knew.

There was a final play in production, the last before Christmas break, George Bernard Shaw's "The Chocolate Soldier." I played the lead, Raina. Nobody ever came but the student body and teachers. We started memorizing our parts, trying on costumes and trying out lighting. I knew Sarah had come back, but we never had too much to say to each other, and I'm not sure I noticed her return. Maybe one day a suitcase by her bed, different clutter in the bathroom, stuff like that. Nothing, like, far out.

I came into our room late one night after our first long dress rehearsal. The lights were out but I could hear breathing, and tiptoed into the bathroom and washed up. I shivered into my pajamas, heavy wool sweater, robe and socks, and fell on the bed. At some point, I looked in Sarah's direction, and all I could see was a lump of blankets. A curled up, hard knot of a lump. Very out of character for my Sarah. It worried me.

❖   ❖   ❖

Sarah came over the next morning at breakfast in the big dining room and sat down with a cup of coffee.

31

"Everything's changed," she said. We didn't talk much or often to each other, unless she was like, getting over on me.

"What changed," I said.

"Do you want my clothes?"

"Sure, Sarah. Like, what are you talking about?"

"You like my clothes?"

I nodded.

"Then you can have them. I'm keeping maybe one or two things. My overcoat...I'm driving to Montpelier. I'm changing my look."

"There's nothing happening in Montpelier but hiking boots, camouflage suits, and army surplus. But, hey, far out."

"I saw a store there. My parents bought me a car." She looked at me for a reaction. "It's all jive."

Sarah studied her coffee cup and set it down, stood up, said she'd see me later, and walked out of the room.

I was eating pancakes. One of the guys from the drama department, my leading man, came over with a tray loaded down with scrambled eggs, toast, and sausage, and joined me.

"Something's afoot with my roomie," I said. "I think it's good, but I'm not sure. I think she's having a radical departure. She just said 'jive' for the first time."

"So, very cool."

"She wants to be hip all of a sudden."

"She won't ever be hip. You're hip. Sarah, if she studies real hard, might some day be cool."

And that was the end of that. We fell into Shaw's characters and cued each other on our lines.

It was late afternoon before I got back to our room. Sarah had emptied her closet and drawers on top of my bed. This was way cool. She had terrific and interesting and beautifully made New York City clothes. As I was mid-exclamation in my thanks, she got up out of her chair and said,

"What do you think?"

Sarah was wearing black and white horizontal striped tights, red cowboy boots, and a short black knit dress that was maybe actually a big sweater. I was pretty shocked.

"Sarah, it that, like, you?"

"It's the new me." She turned around. "Look! It's all gone!"

She had cut off all her hair, to just above her ears. She had a nice face, our Sarah, not a great beauty, but pretty. But this was wildness. Her thick curly hair, and she hadn't done all that bad a job, stuck out sideways from her head. Frankly, it made her a lot more interesting.

"Sit down a minute. I have something to say."

I dropped obediently on the load of clothes.

"Are you okay, Sarah? You're sure acting different. Why'd you cut off all your hair? Your parents are going to kill you! I mean, like, oh man! Sarah!"

"Everything's changed. My parents have gotten a divorce. They did it last week without consulting me, and as far as I'm concerned, I no longer owe them anything. I've been slaving away this year, and all through high school, qualifying for scholarships and straight A's and perfect SATs. Why did I bother? The least they could've done for me is to stay married. I don't think I'd have stayed here, I don't think Vermont or the school is worth four years. Maybe two, then I planned to get my doctorate at Columbia. All the men in my family went to Columbia. Anyway, hair is jive."

She looked genuinely sad. I wasn't used to seeing that on her. I felt bad for Sarah. Her nose started running, but she shut it all down.

"I know I'm not always the easiest person to get along with," Sarah sniffed. (Is that what she thought? I thought she just hated me.) "Everything's turned upside down. I'm going to start living my own life, which I haven't been doing, ever. There's nobody to owe. This is a major sin against me. I will not for one minute more be the perfect daughter." She got up and blew her nose and flushed the tissue. From the bathroom door with the glow of light behind her, she said, "I need a boyfriend. I'm supposed to wait until I'm twenty to date. I never had a boyfriend. How do you go about it."

My jaw must've been on my knees. I had spent my own study time investigating the opposite sex, and it had been pretty clear that Sarah didn't think much of my pursuits or hedonism.

33

Now I was being asked for guidance. That was like, whoa. Way mysterious.

"Are you serious?"

"I want a particular one. He's tall and blond, I think his name is Adrian. I choose him. He lives in Florida. He's very beautiful. I think he would be just about perfect, and I've never seen him with another student, a girl. I talked to him today for the first time. He likes my hair." Sarah looked at her red boots. "And my boots. It's all just jive, anyway."

"I know exactly who you mean," I said, "and yes he'd be great. I mean, I guess he'd be great, I don't know him either, but I'd say he was open to a girlfriend. He keeps to himself, doesn't he, does his own thing, whatever that is. I talked to him once in the dining room. Uh, he's named after a pope, Sarah."

"It doesn't matter. Will you help me? You have to help me. In trade for the clothes. I want Adrian to fall in love with me but I only have two weeks."

"Ten days," I said. "Sure."

I shifted on my bed. One of my favorite sweaters of Sarah's that I'd never had the courage to ask to borrow had fallen next to my foot. I picked it up and held it in front of me. Black cashmere.

"You're giving me this?"

❖   ❖   ❖

Adrian was hard to corner. He was comfortable with himself, very athletic and good looking, platinum blond hair growing out from dark roots but enough still visible to imagine a life spent on the sunny beaches of Miami. He seemed bright, not much interested in conversation, and read a lot. He didn't stay in one place long and disappeared to somewhere unknown with his arms full of books. But the school's campus was small. And there were under a hundred of us, eighty something, and twenty-five teachers. Except for the cook who lived in town, the student body handled the custodial duties. There may have been a maintenance man who made sure the boilers were working and the roofs were mended. There probably was. Getting lost or being invisible wasn't likely to happen, and we were all so excited to meet and get to know each other, there was much more of that going on. The other main option for escape was the little grocery store in town, run by suspicious and resentful townies, but we spent big. The town itself wasn't much bigger than the college. Unless you planned a jaunt that started with a car and a map, you stayed on the old farmstead that housed us all, watching spectacular Vermont skies and staring at the unbelievable color the leaves became.

So my detective work had few complications. My plan, my for-hire expertise, boiled down to some nonchalant stalking of Adrian to see where he went and have Sarah bump into him and start a conversation. She was a prolific reader. She'd most likely know the author or content of whatever Adrian was carrying around. I brushed off Sarah's embarrassment at my approach to snaring the male of the species. For one thing, I didn't mind seeing her a little uncomfortable. For another, the scheme had always worked for me.

But in the middle of trying to sell her on it, we were surprised by seeing Adrian, alone and splendid, on the road to town. Plan B! Get the car, drive by, and offer him a lift. And please, I said on the run next to Sarah, stop saying jive.

I stood behind a tree and held my breath. Adrian leaned in to listen to Sarah, thought about it for a minute, then opened the car door and got in. We scored.

❖   ❖   ❖

Each night for the next week, Sarah came back to our shared room later and later. She put on being friendlier, but I could tell it was a stretch. She must have been moving right along with poor old Adrian. Her exploration of costuming continued, and I had introduced her to the theatre wardrobe room from which she borrowed heavily. She would only say about the now and future conquest, the Miami god, that it ws "progressing." Okay, far out.

Sunday, after a late sleep, warm and cozy under blankets and watching the sun splash around the barren trees outside my window, I forced myself to get up and dressed against the cold. I grabbed a bag of cookies from our stash, not minding that I'd missed breakfast by hours, and not wanting to go outside.

As Sarah came through the door all rosy cheeked and bright-eyed, I noticed for the first time she hadn't been in bed at all, not in our room.

She sat in her rocking chair and pushed herself in a lulling way, the style of the old grannies we'd seen on Vermont porches. She wasn't looking quite happy, it was more the way her face contorted after acing a tennis match. Very matter of fact, she said, "Adrian proposed." And without dropping a stitch, "Think we can still get breakfast?"

Well, Adrian proposed all right. He proposed they go to Sarasota over winter break. There was a friend he knew with a house, probably empty, where they could stay. Sarah had the new Volkswagen Beetle. They'd drive that. If they pooled their money, they could cover gas to Florida and then find jobs.

It sounded great to me. Not only a warm sunny place, but a warm sunny guy, and a working car. And a new burgeoning look for Sarah to try out. And she'd get a tan! Is that, like, cool, or what?

She gave me my instructions, but it was no longer the meticulous Sarah setting a plan in concrete. If her parents demanded to speak to her and got really angry, I was to call her first, short of confession, and she'd deal with it. It was rock solid. We even rehearsed. But I was leaving for California and Sarah didn't have a phone number.

Two weeks before Christmas, after a brief visit with my father and his new wife which didn't do any of us any good, I boarded a Greyhound bus in Boston and settled in for a miserable ride across America. I was sick with a rotten cold. The driver made me go from my choice seat behind his chair to the rear of the bus. He refused to have his head sneezed on for three thousand miles.

❖ ❖ ❖

Two days before January turned into February, I flew back to Vermont. Sarah was back, too, but booked with another roomie. I had the old room to myself. A new student from Europe was expected in a month, and we'd share. It was a week or more before I ran into Sarah. I'd started attending classes, and we saw each other, of all places, in the library, and went for a walk. It was an unusually warm January day, with full sun bouncing off the snow on the ground. Sarah was deeply tanned. And platinum blond.

"You won't believe what I've been doing! Like, no jive!"

"You're in love!" I always hoped for people to be in love.

"Yes, no, I don't know, not that, it's that I joined the circus! Can you dig it?"

Today, rebellious teens pierce their bodies and get tattoos. In those days, we did things.

"I don't believe it!" I didn't believe that she was actually talking to me, either.

"The Ringling Brothers, Barnum and Bailey! They're all set up in Sarasota, it's their home base! I learned how to fly on a trapeze and catch...we both did! You should see Adrian in white tights! First we were apprentices, and God! I got to wear tutus and ballet slippers, oh my God! They have a school, and we enrolled and we performed! Three times! Oh God it was fantastic!"

It sure outdid anything I'd thought of in the past two months. And I got the dig, outperforming me, and in a circus no less. She'd never once come to any of the plays I was in at school.

It wasn't all roses. Adrian's family was very unhappy about his cohabitation with a New York Jewish chick. They were very unhappy to meet her. They were so perfectly miserable they promised to disown Adrian. It turned out he was Adrian the Fourth, in line for something big time.

But Adrian stuck by Sarah. They did find that friend's house and didn't have to pay rent. The circus took up all their time, and they never got jobs, and borrowed food and gas money from everybody they ever met, and sometimes panhandled on the beach. Which was half cool and half uncool, but it got them through. Who cared. Dig it, a circus!

37

"Of course," Sarah added, "there was always a net."

I couldn't help it. I smirked.

We were getting cold, but the news was hot and we kept walking. Sarah said, one day they were drifting down a big Sarasota street drooling at the food in the shops and trying to figure out how to stretch the last five bucks into a month of eats. They passed a bakery, and Adrian recognized the baker from high school. Once inside and talking over free jelly donuts, he described their dilemma.

"You can live a long time," the baker said, "on cake."

"It would have to be," Sarah said, "some huge cake."

"I'm selling a huge cake," the baker said. "Very cheap."

After which, for their last five dollars and $2.50 more they promised to deliver in a week, Sarah and Adrian drove home with a nine-tiered wedding cake that had never been collected, because the bride and groom had soured on each other. A week had passed and it hadn't sold. The icing was so thick, the inside was nearly fresh. It kept the two of them alive for four weeks, though Sarah said she was off sugar for the rest of her life. She also decided it meant they were married.

"Adrian's family wasn't very nice to me. But I'm going to marry him for real. In a church."

She looked like she'd aced another tennis match.

"Then you are in love! Let's have a party or do something."

"I'd just as soon nobody found out, okay? He's not really very bright. But he's very rich. No jive."

At that point, Sarah sort of caught herself up that she was treating me like a friend, and I could see my old roommate again under the tan and electrifying top. The new Sarah bounced off to her car, got in, never looked back, and went somewhere.

❖   ❖   ❖

By summer we had all gone our separate ways. Two years later I was living in a New York City apartment on the Lower East Side, one room, tub in the kitchen. I met Sarah out of the blue in

Thompkins Square Park. Her hair was long and chestnut again, and she was living with her mother. She didn't look bright or solid anymore, or smug. And I'd have bet that she didn't sleep with her arms folded behind her head anymore, either. We went to my place for a cup of coffee, and she asked me if she could use my bathroom, to shoot up. Sarah had just scored some heroin from a dealer in the park. I told her no. She wouldn't talk, and left, to find an alley, I guess, to probe her veins and fill herself with junk.

She'd been well-dressed again, like she used to be, in a fabulous winter coat right out of Vogue and knee-high leather boots. Her hair was still thick and shiny. But there didn't seem to be anything shiny left inside.

❖   ❖   ❖

It's hard enough to think about at all. She was so geared to make it big, either in a career or marriage or both. Sarah was orderly and scholarly and disciplined. What Sarah went after, Sarah got, whether it was Adrian or a doctorate from Columbia or a high wire act. What she never went after and never got was independence but she never once chose to do anything alone. Still, why hadn't her great Florida revolution been a breakthrough, something to seize upon, to alter her life for all time. I had a cry after she left, shaking, not understanding any of it having gone so wrong for her.

My own nights were spent painting canvases. My days in miserable jobs, midtown Manhattan. I'd visit Off Broadway theatre groups and the gypsy performers on the Lower East Side. Sometimes I'd paint a backdrop, or teach a class on moulage and make-up. I was surprised I'd learned so much at school, but it seeped in. New York City was the Emerald City to me, pulsing with life in forms I'd never encountered before. I was damned scared and damn happy, sure I was making a mess of my life and that I didn't know what I was doing, only that I wanted more of all of it.

I remained obstinate, no good at being tied down, and getting to like being a loner. Eventually, I stopped talking to either coastal parent.

I still couldn't be told what to do, and got fired a lot for my arrogance. I suffered enough for it to put myself in therapy. While I was sorting out the many things wrong with me, new jobs were as easy to find in that big town as walking through a door, even if you'd been an idiot on the last one. I kept going, in spite of myself, and made a lot of mistakes, but started to learn from them for the first time in my life. It was a crooked path, but it was the one I chose.

I thought after she walked out of my apartment, where's the fight in her gone? Sarah always pushed herself so hard. Where's the fight gone? And then I realized, Sarah never had any fight that she could call her own. It was always in reaction to somebody else, or their expectations, or their criticism. Whoever she was getting even with now, it seemed to be working for her. Very uncool, Sarah. No jive.

III

Midnight Manhattan

Midnight Manhattan

It was a winter twenty years ago in New York City, and I'm guessing, because it was nippy but not snowy, that it was November. My son Trevor was four. I had suggested and he had accepted a trip to midtown for a movie. Off we went.

The subway left us nearby. We arrived on the F train, in the vicinity of St. Patrick's Cathedral. The movie house we were headed to was the Fifth Avenue Cinema, and the eleven pm showing of Disney's One Hundred and One Dalmatians. We had a few blocks to walk.

The store windows never failed to engage. As for the movie, if we didn't make the beginning, we'd sit through the start after it rolled again. If it was the last show, we'd be just as happy. Movies of any duration were a treat. More, for some reason, then, than now. And with a young boy and his mother doing the raising alone, we were always late for everything. Fifth Avenue Christmas windows were worth stalling to see.

So we walked and stopped and dawdled, bundled up good on the empty winter sidewalks, me lifting Trevor to better see the giddy colors and shapes behind the spotless glass. There are parts of Fifth Avenue that have a corridor effect and it made us aware of our small size to look up at the gray brown stone facades that loomed high around us that night. Street lamps lit splotches of concrete with military precision. Building glass, polished chrome, and marble, and brass all impeccably tended. It had a calming effect on the two Brooklynites who lived in disorderly chaos with cats and dogs in a roughshod old apartment, on a street splattered with graffiti. Yes indeedy we were way uptown. I stood a little taller and made a neater bow of Trevor's scarf. A block from the theatre, we could see the marquee.

"We'll buy popcorn, Trev. I've got enough to get us in, and buy popcorn."

He laughed and rubbed his hands together. The holiday weeks of waitressing had left a bulge in my wallet.

43

Excuse me," said a suddenly present and polite child of about ten at my side.

"Hello!" I said.

Then the ten year old just stood watching first Trevor, then me. I wasn't sure what he expected but he expected something. He had dark hair, dark eyes, and a tidiness to him, but was not dressed for the cold. To my son, this was a big boy. And in the rigid prejudices of children, who decide in a flash if another child is important, this one was way old. Trevor immediately looked around for something to please him.

I asked the boy if he was lost.

"No."

"Okay. Uh, we're going to a movie. It's about to start."

No reaction.

"Where are your parents?"

No reaction.

For me, growing up is still a long, somewhat bizarre experience. I may never come to grips with being the grownup. I tend to treat everyone as equal in age. But of course we're not, and he was small, and unformed, and needy. I looked around for help on the quiet street. Only a handful of cars went by, and none were parked, and the sidewalk was very empty of other people.

"What's your name?" I asked him, thinking it a good place to start. I was prancing to keep my feet warm, and slapping my sides, which Trevor imitated with more invention, including a zooming airplane effect.

The quiet child fessed up.

"My name is Mark."

"Aren't you cold? You don't have a warm enough jacket on. Where do you live, Mark?"

I took off my scarf and wrapped it around his red to blue neck.

"I live in Connecticut."

"How did you get here?"

"I took the train."

Well, it went on like this for a few minutes, and I admit to looking harder for some sign of a parent or guardian or guardian angel who would come forth. But I'd been doing that my whole life, and they don't always materialize when you need them. Then Mark said he guessed he'd run away from home.

"Were they mean to you? Did somebody beat you or something?"

What do you ask? Huckleberry Finn and Tom Sawyer built a raft and went off to live the pirate's life because grownups made them wear shoes and swallow awful medicine. It doesn't take much to think you'd be better off elsewhere.

"Nobody beat me or anything," said Mark, and did not appear wounded or undernourished. He was well dressed and clean, a little trembly of the lip, and cold.

"I'm on the way to...that theatre," I pointed, "and we're going to see One Hundred and One Dalmatians. It'll be warm inside. Ever seen it?"

"No."

"Want to?"

"I guess so."

Mark's confidence in my ability to take the lead helped. At least he hadn't said, "Are you nuts? That's too stupid for words!" Though maybe it was.

"Then come on, I have enough for two popcorns."

We went in, to an empty house, got good up-front seats which Trevor and I liked, and Mark from Connecticut was okay with. The boys each held their own buttered popcorns, and I got Milk Duds, because I refused to see a movie without them.

Trevor was asleep before Cruella DaVil hit the screen. It was toasty inside. The animation was superb. Every now and then I'd sneak a look at Mark, and he was absorbed and doing fine. He ate all his popcorn, and then Trevor's.

The credits rolled, we bundled back into scarves and mittens and stocking caps and the three of us were outside under the theatre canopy, getting used to the night, watching the fog from our breathing as doors were locked and lights went out behind us. I insisted Mark keep the scarf wrapped around his neck, and tried to lift it to his red ears. We liked the movie. Trevor was way past needing bed.

"Mark, we're heading back to Brooklyn. I don't think it would be such a great idea to bring you along, I mean, it's probably illegal and where would I put you? I'm poor right now, I have a lot of plans to change that but I don't think I could feed another mouth. For the minute here, I think we have to figure out how to get you back to New England."

"Where's that?"

"That's where you live."

"Oh."

"I see it this way, Mark. Home maybe wasn't so bad, just something boiled over inside you, and you needed to take off. It's a tradition with American kids." I patted his shoulder, a kind of congratulatory thing. "Maybe when you're back, you can figure out how to stand it a little better. Before you even know it, you'll be on your own! I left home when I was fifteen," (I lied outright, it was seventeen but I wanted to give him ready hope), "and some kids move out even sooner than that! Why don't you wait til you can handle it better."

Mark was taking it in. Considering the case I was trying to make.

I was holding Trevor against my shoulder and chest and he was gone to the world. His sweet, still-babied breath was making a hot spot on my neck and it was soothing us both. I hugged Mark against my side for a minute, but he didn't respond comfortably. Okay, he doesn't need a hug.

"What do you think, Mark. Feeling a little better about going home?"

Then Mark was trying not to cry. But it wasn't powerful in him, more bracing up, I thought, for the inevitable meet-up with parents. I had no idea how long he'd been gone. He was not wild-eyed with fear. More a kid who'd taken a gamble, to see what was up in New York City, and God bless his adventuring heart, I hoped he'd be up for a lot more of it in years to come.

We shuffled and wiggled our way toward the subway we'd come from, and were now opposite St. Patrick's Cathedral again. I got this bright idea. We would cross the street, and knock, and Bing Crosby himself would open the door and lead us into a warm room with a fire going and sit down at the piano and sing us a song! I took Mark's hand, and we crossed the entirely unpeopled Fifth Avenue to the huge front entrance of thick wood and black

47

iron hinges. We sidled past it to a small portal off to the side, with rocks uniform on the path and a garden around it. I knocked.

We stood expectantly. I knocked again, louder.

"Are you Catholic, Mark?"

"I don't think so," he whispered to me.

"You'd probably know,' I said. "Neither am I."

Finally, a priest came to the door and opened it but not far, though I could see his full length and his cassock. There was a dim light behind him, and it was not possible to see his face or his expression.

He was a tall, slim man, this St. Patrick's caretaker, an El Greco kind of shape, the wind and cold at play around his black hems. There was a smell to the air that drew out and around him from the old stone church, a sanctified smell from another century, howling with rituals unknown to me.

"Father, uh, if that's right, uh, this little boy was out here on Fifth Avenue, and well, I can't do much for him, and I have my boy to worry about, this young man is named Mark," I smiled at Mark and was suddenly pleased at this obvious belonging, called the same as a disciple, for goodness sake! "And it appears he's run away from home. From Connecticut."

For the first time, it seemed like a secret and I'd let the cat out of the bag, and had no idea how my confession was going to be received. I felt guilty of everything, ready for hell to descend on all our heads. I needn't have worried.

"We don't help with that,' said the priest, half the words lost to the closing door and darkness. I packed enough umbrage to carry us right back across the street, and put the cathedral at our backs.

"So much for Bing Crosby, kid," I said.

Oddly enough, and for the first time, Mark was smiling. His child's face was wearing some happiness, that depositing him with just any figure of authority was not going to be a piece of cake. Maybe it was a clue to the Connecticut problem, something going on to unload this quiet boy, a split in the family? I had no idea. But oh, Mark, don't let it get to you. So much of that ahead, hearts filled up with trumpets, and hearts torn to pieces.

We were closing in on one in the morning. I spotted a New York City police officer a block ahead of us. He was in one of those big dark blue wool, double-breasted, brass-buttoned overcoats. He was on the young side, and looked friendly. I shifted Trevor to hold his limp sleeping weight, and had the runaway in tow.

"Officer! Officer!"

I'd always liked cops. There was one who used to cross me to school in Emerson, New Jersey, at my start of first grade. Cops were protective, and did damage control, and crisis management.

I got the story out fast, saying after the intro that Mark here seemed to have taken the day off from Connecticut, that he was fine and had a movie and popcorn in him, and it was the extent of my resourcefulness. At some point, the cop had stopped listening to me, thanked me, patted Trevor on the head, put his fine large arm around Mark, and they headed downtown. Smiling pink cheeks were visible on both their profiles. The grownup seemed to be asking Mark questions in the most sensible, adult way, without a thought more for the Brooklynites. I smiled. They were going to be inside a warm precinct and Mark was in for a hot dog and ice cream, which, in every Daily News story about such things, the New York City Police Department guarantees.

Trevor was like a hot water bottle, fast asleep against me, all steamy exhales and baby gurgles. I pulled his cap to better cover his little head. And I wondered if the boy-child in my arms would spurn this motherly fuss, get on a train, and see Connecticut in six years.

New York City is a magic box of remarkable moments that opens up over and over again.

Nobody was on Fifth Avenue but us. Steam puffed out of the tops of buildings that shot up on either side, too far off to see, as if they were celestial locomotive stacks with the engines revving. There was Bergdorf's department store and Saks at eye level, dazzle and razzle from their Christmas windows. The lighting was unobtrusive and gentle. Tiffany's windows were glowing, and warm and inviting.

We turned the corner and walked past a man in front of the Tiffany display on the other side. He was a businessman, in a quality camel coat, with an expensive silk paisley scarf at his throat. It must've been comfortably warm, for his coat hung open and he had a good dark suit and bright white shirt under it. His haircut was the kind regularly tended to by a barber who knows what he's doing. But the man was agitated, and his leather gloved fists were clenched, and he looked upset on his fine, clean-shaven face.

He turned when we passed by, and blurted out, "I need a diamond ring! I have to get a diamond ring!" and looked back into that soul of gold and gems, just out of reach. "Where can I get a diamond ring, do you know? I need it now, I need it tonight! Oh God! Isn't anything open!"

There sure was a lot of variety in the prayers said on Fifth Avenue that night.

"I have no idea, mister. Even in New York City at this time night? No, I have no idea, sorry."

"I have to! I have to! I have to!" he said to the window.

It struck me very curious. I didn't know anybody, not in my life at the moment anyway, who'd be in such a swivet over me on Fifth Avenue in the middle of the night.

We had a long trip ahead of us, and probably a good wait for the train to pull into the station. Home was far away, and this man and his alien trouble with diamonds served to set a gap between me and uptown I hadn't felt all night. Some fabulous female, manicured and pedicured, was waiting somewhere, hand extended, toes tapping in irritation, for her desperate guy to come back with a question to pop and a token of romance in a black velvet box. He was so worked up! Compared to the Disney dalmatians and the little boy lost from Connecticut and the child in my arms, and the popcorn for two and Milk Duds and getting three of us into a movie in one night plus roundtrip subway fare, his life looked way too easy. I wasn't past feeling a little smug. I even felt more grown up. The diamond-desperate fellow was living a life not as interesting as my own.

I wouldn't have treated him that way, for one thing. It wasn't much of a quest the girl of his dreams had set for him, and he was up for a bad time, was my guess, and not just this one midnight in Manhattan.

Now young Mark, there was a guy who knew how to have a good night out on the town. And if he knew it at ten, he probably wouldn't be wasting his time when he was full-grown on a silly girl who expected silly things of him, no indeed! If Mark ever did need a diamond, he'd get on a train and go right to the mine for it, and unearth it himself! And my son, Trevor, he'd be full of adventure too, like his mom. The three of us could run circles around this Fifth Avenue swell, and we knew how to spend a Sunday night in New York City, uptown, and none of it was silly.

"She's all wrong for you," I said to the man.

I hoped the midnight winter air would clear his brain, but wouldn't have bet on it. Not a bad guy, I was sort of rooting for him. Maybe a little on the dutiful side, you know, conventional. He knew how to pick a winter coat, though. We had a subway to catch.

IV

Rodin of the Blue Ridge

Rodin of the Blue Ridge

I hadn't lived more than two weeks that summer in the Blue Ridge Mountains before dogs came visiting from other houses, near and far.

Most dogs were free runners in the woods of Virginia, dogs of any good size to them. Land was still cheap and most property had a minimum of twenty acres and five hundred was common, and the dogs owned the land.

I'd been unpacking paintings and books and hanging things on the walls. The sound of splashing brought me out the door. There wasn't any water near the house.

I nearly got bowled over by a tri-colored streak, three huge dogs chasing each other, half-soaked and obviously having a good time. I hadn't found the full rain barrels under each corner spout yet, saved for drought (it never happened), or when the well went off in power outages (it happened all the time). I backed up on the porch steps to enjoy the show.

One was a big brown Labrador, with a massive squared kind of head. The other, a pale white-blond female Lab; and finally, thinner and maybe younger, but robust as the others, a black and glossy boy, also Lab. They obviously knew my new home better than I did.

Like a lot of Virginia houses, a rail fence with two or three tiers circled the groomed land, with stone walled farmland, pastures and paddocks beyond. The dogs leapt my fence, and rushed through the woods and fields, circled back and dove in the barrels. They snapped at each other's ankles and rolled in the grass. They were a riot of happy life. Not one of them would slow down to be petted. They had too much to do. I went back inside, pleased at the company and interruption, and an hour or so later, noticed they had gone.

The dog visits were apparently Sunday specials. I forgot about them with setting up my studio, but the next Sunday they were back; and the Sundays after that, I looked for them, doggy biscuits at the ready.

55

By the next month, the large chocolate Lab was coming on his own, midweek; I'd find him on the lawn early in the morning, waiting for me to put in an appearance. I confess that at first I thought him too angular, and ugly. There were show dogs, and there were rescued dogs in New York. In between are what I always called fire escape dogs, the ones who were black and white, round as sausages on short legs, invariably named Bootsie, and panting on fire escapes in the summer. My last dog had been a spectacular white and tan German shepherd with perfect markings and features. I'd found her tied in temporary care in a neighbor's yard. But I'd had plenty of Bootsies in my life. I guess my eyes just weren't used to the configuration of this large, square-headed dog. He didn't fit any familiar picture I had in my head. But I was flattered that I'd been chosen by him as one worthy of visits and curiosity.

The chocolate Lab was younger than I'd first thought, maybe three or four. He had a blue collar, which I couldn't get close enough to read. He let me pet him, not for more than a few strokes, and when he looked at me he had a gaze I can only describe as important, and a very generous heart, which somehow was immediately clear. He didn't trust containment. Nor did he trust being held by the collar. But he did like a pet on the head, and had started, before long, to lean against my leg for a minute or two before taking off.

The visits remained erratic. Sometimes he'd come covered in mud, so we played a game with the hose. The days were infernally hot and muggy. He wouldn't put up with a bath, but he liked a squirt. If I aimed the hose steady in one direction, he'd charge through it. I got as far as the start of a shampoo once, but he got away before the final rinse. I figured he'd work it out. We weren't far from the Shenandoah River or its tributaries downhill.

The Lab still made it on Sundays with his pals. My landlord said that the two of them lived a mile away, and I met their humans who, one Sunday at sunset, came to collect them. We got into a routine of my phoning them if the dogs were still at my place at dusk. But the big chocolate was a mystery. Nobody knew where he lived. For sure, the blond was his wife and the shiny black youngster, their son. Chocolate Labs, as I understand it, can't be bred. They are a special mix of canine alchemy, and not even two chocolates guarantee brown pups. Wherever dad took off from, remained his business. He had his ways.

By October, the weather was changing fast, and the forest turning a gray brown, flowers dying off and rainfall steady. I saw the Labrador one or two times but he wasn't visiting as frequently. And never, any more, on Sunday.

One clear day, I went out to watch the dawn, a promising display of rose-topped and gray-bottomed clouds, a gold filigree at their edges. I could hear a rustling in the woods on the far side of my gate. It took me some time to track the source. I had grown accustomed to the predators of New York City but wasn't sure yet how to deal with mountain lions, bobcats, and black bear. But it was my friend, the chocolate Lab, and he had returned with a new friend of his, a full size, very black, standard poodle, in full regalia pet shop groom. God knows what they talked about, but the two lay on their bellys, chins to front paws, watching me. The Lab seemed pleased and excited that I'd shown up for display, and made a few comments to the newcomer. They were gossiping about me! But they stayed put, out of reach, on the far side of the fence. It was very funny. I got dog biscuits, which they accepted. By the time I'd gotten back out with bowls of dog food I'd laid in for just such a moment, they had gone. I never did see the poodle again. He was quite splendid.

❖   ❖   ❖

I had, at that moment on my journey, mixed feelings about new dogs. I still had many cats sequestered away in secret in the house. My outlaws. I'd had to sign a lease with the names and descriptions of the two cats I did claim, and carefully noted the most common color, orange-white. On one visit, the realtor said, "Look how that cat is following us to every window around the house!" I said, yes, clever cat, and knew it was at least six of the twenty. Fraud on behalf of little creatures is a virtue. When I moved from Brooklyn, I'd found, reluctantly, homes for the last three of my rescued dogs, and they were good adoptions. Two years before I left New York, both my German Shepherds had died within months of each other from cancers. That was my Bambi; and my Skooter, who I described. We'd had ten lively years. Bambi was part wolf. Skooter was a movie star.

I wasn't sure I wanted a dog yet. I was no longer a homeowner, but a renter, my life considerably changed. I was in the throes of an experiment at long last, the adventure of the wilds finally at hand after decades of my wanting it to be so. I wasn't sure how long I'd stay anywhere. I planned to try and make a living full time with my chosen compulsions: sculpting, painting, and writing. I didn't have a clue about what lay ahead. Or if I could care for one more fuzzy person, no matter how interesting the chocolate Lab was.

❖   ❖   ❖

Several weeks went by and I didn't see much of the dog. I figured that fate had made my mind up. I got past being concerned for him because he'd lived his life on that mountain. I was pretty sure he was okay.

Winter was upon us. We'd had several good snows and the days rarely reached twenty degrees. I had firewood to chop and forays down to the Food Lion in town when the roads cleared. New experiences with wilderness occupied me, too.

I'd discovered turkeys fly, and roost in trees. That vultures, eagles, and hawks shared my mountain. That the big red fox were wily and fleet. That the screech owl's cry was more earsplitting and chilling than a souped-up speaker-filled car suddenly parking on your Brooklyn block.

❖   ❖   ❖

A few days before Thanksgiving I went on to the skating rink my front lawn had become. I tasted the snow falling from the skies and headed down the perilous gravel drive, barely visible this day, as it passed through two miles of trees to the main road that bisected the mountain.

Something large and slow was moving up the hill toward me. It startled me. The woods had plenty of large things living in it, and my eyesight wasn't so good. Whatever it was stayed about a hundred feet away, saw me, and then in an almost painful listing from side to side, kept coming. In a second, I realized it was the chocolate Lab of the summer days and early fall.

I ran to him, and the minute I reached him he collapsed at my feet. He looked at me balefully; his eyes drooped down to his jowls, and were very white. I screamed at this sight, so disabled, my old friend. I was sure he'd been hit by a car or truck or wounded by a wild animal. I pulled off my mittens and traced his body for blood as he lay on my boots.

He was horribly bumpy…bee stings?…in winter? I pulled and encouraged him to his feet and half carried him back home, both of us rigid from the cold penetrating gray sky, lowered by the new storm overhead.

I had a screened porch. The dog, as before, was reluctant to go on it but finally let me bring him through the door, though no tempting or pleading could get him inside to comfort, safety, where a fire blazed and light poured warmly to us and Beethoven blasted from the radio. I yanked a blanket off the wicker chair and got the dog to lie down, and covered him. I cried at the sight of him. Part fear in me, part desperate at the thought of vet bills, and a car that wouldn't start. The emergency of him faced me, his ribs poking every touch, his eyes glazed and white as chalk.

I ran into the kitchen, (latching the screen door as a precaution against a possible panicked search for him later in the woods), where I mixed four egg yolks in a bowl of milk, and brought it to him. He lapped up most of it. I had never been able to get this close for this long. The ministering to him was anxious for him and me, and I thought him trusting and brave to put up with it.

Snow was blowing onto the porch, but still he fought against being taken inside. I spent my energy piling cardboard against the screens, holding it up with boxes and porch furniture. I tried to make some idea I had of a safe spot. The dog food dish was next to his face, and he made a few stabs but didn't have the energy to chew. I was struck by his complete exhaustion. Had he run away from some far miles off, and remembered me? He could not hold up his head. I'd pulled a wool blanket off my bed and covered us both, petting him and talking, being allowed now to inspect the bumps that covered his body. I hadn't seen him in a while, but surely not more than three weeks had really passed. What had happened to his vigorous life-loving dog?

Ticks. He was covered with ticks. They were huge and swollen with his blood, not more than half an inch apart or clustered, horrible ticks. I could see now they hung off his ears and lips, and were buried in his chest and back haunches and forelegs. I had never seen an infestation like it in my life. Frantically, I started pulling them out. I knew a right and wrong way to extract predatory insects but the hell with procedure. The dog was being exsanguinated before my eyes. It explained the absence of color on him, the white, blank, dry gums. My only hope was that his previous strength would carry him. In a short time, I'd reached ninety ticks and stopped counting. He was asleep on my lap now and breathing more easily. The honor I'd been bestowed made me cry. And I would come to know that his judgement in all things was usually right.

I pulled at the blanket on and under him, and found it soaked through. He'd urinated freely, too weak to move. I kissed his head and told him not to mind.

The filthy ticks went into the fire inside. They wouldn't pull this again. I added more firewood and tried to warm up, watching the dog through the windowed door. None of the ticks had gotten on me. They'd been sated, no longer searching for fresh blood.

The Labrador hadn't moved. I had tried pulling him inside on the blanket, but he snarled and got up enough energy to show he'd bite if I persisted, then looked sorry for it. If he'd lived through winters like this before, maybe he'd survive with the blanket. I'd never once felt sorry for him before this day. He'd always looked so in charge.

There's a standard to the size of things in sculpting; half size the object; quarter size; or life size; and twice or three times life size, is heroic. This dog, ill or not, was heroic size, and so was his character.

Right then, I only wanted him to live. Maybe we'd get a vet later. I was peeved at my inability to get him settled in the big warm country kitchen where I'd gone again to mix eggs and milk, the last of both, a couple of good sized tablespoons of honey, and half shot of Jack Daniel's. I beat it all in a saucepan and warmed it up. Back on the freezing porch I tilted his head to it, and he slid his tongue into the brew, pulling it into him till the bowl was empty.

The storm had intensified, snow blowing in sideways on us. When I felt it safe to leave him, I stapled bed sheets and raw canvas against the wooden frames of the porch, nearly useless in a few minutes. The mountain roads would be long closed by now. I'd had that much winter to know the drill. We were going to have to come through this alone. He gulped down some water. The sun had gone.

I found a small heater in an unpacked box and set it up next to us. The porch was arctic, the circle around us some oddball oasis. I split the seams of a large cardboard box and tented the pooch. He insisted with his waning strength that his head and paws be left exposed. He wanted to be ready to bolt. I replaced the blanket with one of my big quilted moving blankets and sat next to him as long as I could in the pool of wet snow migrating from the ring of heat. I'd propped the heater on a layer of bricks, so we wouldn't be electrocuted.

It was five below zero. I still couldn't get him indoors, and gave up pushing for it. His body had warmed up. By midnight I couldn't stand it for myself. My hands and feet were numb. I ran inside to the fire, got out of my wet clothes and found some dry sweat pants and a flannel shirt, and a dry sweater. It made me as happy as if I'd been pulled out after a Channel swim into a dry boat. I curled up under a comforter, shivering on the couch, but got up every few minutes to check on him. Thank God I'd gotten the cats fed early, before I'd even found the dog, and they were all comfortable on coverlets and beds. My cats always went into some kind of false hibernation when the weather turned bad, as if they were in for a long sleep. But they'd respond to heat like lizards, and to sunshine like geraniums.

The dog was sleeping deeply at last. I gently rolled back his muzzle and shined a flashlight on his gums. The palest pink was visible. He sighed and I think recognized that I was petting him though he didn't open his eyes. Twelve hours had gone by, and I thought maybe the crisis was over. His breathing was regular. He'd stopped shaking. I cursed the Virginia ticks.

I don't know how long I slept, or he'd slept, but when I came to, it was because of his barking. And his food dish was empty.

The chocolate Lab, looking more revived that I'd hoped for, did a nose to tail shake and woofed. I'd have sworn he was smiling. He took a few steps and, surprised at his own drained strength, sat immediately. He was in the same position when I stormed back with a can of dog food frantically opening it and he nearly ate it out of the can.

Then he wanted to go out! It was pitch black and the wind was still in an uproar, but I didn't want to deny him anything. I walked next to him, steadying him against my leg. He didn't go more than fifteen feet, emptied his bladder, and thrilled me by heading back to the porch. He sat and watched me make up a fresh bed for him. The snow had stopped falling.

I held open the door to the house again, but the Labrador stood his ground mid-porch, and looked a little sad that he was frustrating me but wouldn't change his mind. Instead, he walked into and curled up under the peculiar cardboard teepee and went back to sleep. I got some olive oil and rubbed his coat. He must've been sore. He had a thick coat of brown and gold and red hairs and a marvelous full tail. It seemed to please him, and he let me fuss a little more, and I did find a few more ticks but after what we'd been through, it was laughable. Hah, ticks! We laugh at you now!

Fresh coffee, bacon and eggs, and maybe toast with honey sounded like something I could no longer live without. Then I realized I was out of eggs, and ended up with a bacon sandwich, and the dog woke up long enough to eat half. He could now chew.

In less than twenty minutes I was curled up on the couch trying to get warm and almost immediately, and gladly, fell asleep.

The dog did not stir much for a full day, beyond his recovered appetite and taking in three large cans of dog food and two forays out to take care of business. I found a few cans of evaporated milk, and some soup, and he had that, too.

I had been up since early afternoon to get my very accommodating cats squared away. Winter continued swirling around us, Bach flute sonatas filling the air. You'd think I could get the dog into all that lovely liveliness, but I could not.

❖   ❖   ❖

I'd taken off his blue nylon collar and had time to inspect it. Someone had written a phone number in laundry marker. I poured myself a cup of coffee. What to do. Considering the shape I'd found him in, maybe his owners would be frantic, suspecting the worst. Or what if (and how would I find out?) what if they'd caused the problem, through neglect or cruelty. I'd have to size them up fast. I would not return him to a nightmare. Once I identified my location and me I wouldn't have a choice if they demanded him back. They could even bring in the sheriff, or animal control, all of which would, as they are known to do, sooner kill than look at him. He was weak and thin. It hadn't been just the ticks. Something dramatic and serious had happened, that he'd even allow such a disaster. I dialed the number on his collar.

"Hello," I said to the voice answering. I used a fake first name and said it fast. "We are apparently sharing a dog."

I was stunned at what unleashed from the other end of the phone. The chocolate Labrador's owner could hardly talk fast enough to cover all the rotten things he had to say about my dog! Over and over and over, he said, 'Don't let him in the house! Never let him in the house!' That the dog was constant trouble. Couldn't be trained. Broke all they tried to tie him with. Lived outdoors all the time. General nuisance, and so on. They only came home on weekends, lived near town at the foot of the mountain, and worked all week in Washington, D.C. Somebody was supposed to be feeding him, but maybe they hadn't, and anyway the dog had no sense and by now I knew whose side I was on. Sometimes you start up a war with a person and all they want after that is a way to get even, so I kept my fury sub rosa, and left off with: "Well, he's here if you want him but I don't mind if he stays all winter." I told him my phone number without giving in to the temptation to change a digit or two. I wanted to keep it legal as I could stand, and was far more polite than I could bear.

By the time I re-cradled the phone I knew there was no way in hell those sonsobitches were ever going to touch my dog again. What lay ahead was convincing the dog.

I went back to him on the porch. The distant sun was setting silver fire to the icy trees. The lawns and pastures and woods beyond were a white foggy mass of barely undulating shapes. It was still way below freezing, maybe zero. I didn't know just how much half-living on the porch all winter I was going to be able to pull off.

Generally, I'm of the mind that you solve a crisis when confronted with it. And more permanent solutions follow close at hand. I couldn't control the attachment I felt after what we'd been through together, or that his other home sounded like hell and a half.

He must've been locked inside some place, and not fed, then finally, starved, gotten free. He had enough sense not to get caught again, maybe, but would he go back? Was there something there to hold him, in his heart. I'd heard the voices of young children in the background of that awful call. And somebody had gone to the trouble to write their phone number on his collar. Maybe just the father didn't like him. Would he tell the family? Would there be a broken-hearted woman or child or grandma. Well, I didn't know any of that. I worked hard for ten minutes at being equitable. It didn't work. I decided that if he'd have me, the chocolate Lab was now mine.

I got washed up, did the dishes and put on another pot of coffee. I went through the house turning on lights against the gloomy dark. I shook the kindling bag out into the fire and headed for the woodpile outside, to tidy the plastic sheet over the firewood. I'd already lived through the experience of using the propane kitchen oven to dry logs. You don't want to make a habit of it. The cords of wood were inside the front gate, about four feet high and twelve feet long.

The chocolate Lab was standing at the porch door and woofed at me. It looked as if he had some of his old strength back. With considerable reluctance, I held open the door. It was an awful moment as I watched him run, a little unsteady but not bad, but run! Away from the house and me! He urinated on the gate (I decided that was significant), then turned around and looked at me. I guess I was stopped in my tracks. The only marks between us in the snow were paws. He let out a string of barks, deep and important. It was a happy sound, then a little bit of a wail. Finally, his head back and lips circled, he let out a genuine howl.

"No," I said, but I said it quietly. Don't take off.

The dog nosed open the gate, and squeezed through the small gap the packed rise of snow allowed, and ran.

I called, "Rodin!" after him. I'd already decided to name him after the sculptor...that massive head and paws so like the artist's...but he ignored me. I watched his progress away and down the hill, and went back inside.

❖   ❖   ❖

A full day passed, and there was no sign of him. The power of the storm lessened, but the electricity had gone out, and utility company road crews were lighting the woods, searching out damaged lines, their amazing beacons of light distorting the dark pre-dawn as they brilliantly bounced off snow and ice.

The sun came out, weakened, barely able to make a dent in the blackened sky. A new storm was due by evening. I hadn't seen the dog for two days.

I bundled up for yet another trek to the firewood pile, determined to make at least five trips and relieve my weary bones from a midnight fetching of more. With the last load for the night in my arms, I turned toward the woods and called to him, in his new name.

"Rodin! Rodin! Chocolate Labrador, where are you? Come on, boy!"

There was neither sight nor sound of him. I went back on the porch, the screen door sticking in a snow bank that I'd have to set right when I emptied my arms. It was a miserable ending, this being left alone after all, and having decided to make room in my house and heart for a dog again.

I was pulling the screen door of the porch from its imprisonment in snow, when Rodin, from absolutely nowhere, rushed past me, through the front door to the house I'd left open, leapt on the couch in front of the fire and, sitting on the blankets, he smiled.

You do imagine things in the woods alone. I spent a part of every day separating fact from fiction, things I'd sworn I'd heard or seen, and hadn't. It's not quite madness, its just part of the life. I looked at the dog on the couch, and wondered if I'd wanted it so badly I was making it up.

Rodin woofed. A real dog's woof, not the sound of a hallucination. And then he smiled, again.

V

Vanguardinia

Vanguardinia

When I first moved to the log cabin in Harper's Ferry, it was through and in and under the worst winter that area had seen for two hundred years.

The farm was ninety acres set back in the civil war hills, a panoply of field and marsh, paths to walk and streams to ford. I rented the land, and the log cabin built on it a century and a half before I got there. It was two stories, surrounded by porches, with a small kitchen and a den, and another room for whatever on the ground floor. The bedroom was in the uppermost peak, to which, thankfully, the heat from the woodstove below rose and nestled. It was isolated and rustic, not easy for the owner to find a tenant for, except at the moment it suited me to a T. I had a remaining family of six Brooklyn cats, and a Labrador.

A large red barn on the property, dating back to the fifties, was built on the foundation of the one before it that had collapsed in years of storms and hearty use. One door was off its hinges. It had a loft. It was clean and dry. An old working John Deere tractor was parked alongside and covered with a blue waterproof tarp.

The loft was used for storage of household things, small machinery, broken bits and parts of who-knew-what in boxes, fixtures, tools, and a family of cats.

At least I thought the cats lived in the top of the barn, but it turned out they had a preference for the subterranean. The first I saw of any of them was the beautiful orange and white girl. I could see she'd been, or was, a recent mother. I came running back to her with tuna and cat chow and milk, but she hissed like mad at me. She ate hungrily. She spit and she threatened. I named her Vixen, on the spot.

At the back of the barn and the start of a staircase to the loft, was flooring of two by fours, raised off the dirt ground by more of the same. On the second or third visit to Vixen, I watched her retreat, not just under the flooring, but down into a tunnel she'd dug, or renovated for her needs from some previous occupant.

There was a tiny newborn kitten's body at the start of the tunnel. It was decomposed by some time. I wondered if a litter remained down deep inside the hole, and listened for their cries at the returning mother. I heard them, muffled squeals, and knew then the family was ongoing, underground.

Within a week, the tiny newcomers were venturing out at feeding time until Vixen's alarming screams drove them scurrying back to safety. I'd seen at least four babies. There might have been more.

❖   ❖   ❖

The Harper's Ferry winter was incredibly bitter, snow up to ten feet on the ground and layers of ice through it, tree branches bent to breaking under the heavy burden, and a day hardly reaching fifteen degrees for nearly two months.

But a new place is always an adventure waiting to be had. There were packed down deer trails to follow, an icehouse of old stone that was fascinating, and a gatehouse filled with farming tools I'd never seen before. My big chocolate Labrador, Rodin, and I tramped the snow over the five hundred feet or so to the barn. I'd left things in there at the time of the move, and made regular treks to retrieve boxes of books, painting materials, chairs, and various parts of my disconnected life. I'd bring meals to the barn cats, after feeding my own inside the cabin. Rodin would patiently wait outside. I slowly got to know Vixen and her family.

I think she started understanding I was on her side because she was hissing less. I did come faithfully and did bring good things for her and her children. She was no longer screaming RETREAT! to them. Vixen stopped gulping down the food, and even spent a few minutes after the meal to groom her pretty self in full view, which I took as a compliment.

I wanted her to trust me, to sit purring in my lap while I petted her. We were a long way off, if it ever happened. This courtship between human and feral animal, every precious movement and sign, had to proceed with care. I relished the daily

contact and small triumphs. My marmalade Vixen, show me your heart, show me your family, and slowly, she did.

Two of the gutsier babies, a boy and a girl like Vixen in coloring, started coming right up to the food dish while I sat about ten feet away. Vixen let them, and stopped being nervous about it. She was putting some weight on, and looked calmer. One of the two, the girl, came to within a foot of me when I opened a tuna can, and got clouted by her mother for it, but only once. After that, she and Vixen came up as a pair, beautiful and identical, mother and child. The little one screamed for her food. She hadn't an ounce of reserve to her now. I called her Vanguardinia, combining her firstliness, and her sweet flower-like self in one name.

❖   ❖   ❖

The seasons started to change. Rain replaced snow. Dawn in the forest was irresistible. If we made it past the trees and out to the meadow through knee-deep mud, we'd see the mists levitating off the new grasses. The early spring brought Orioles and heron and geese to the marsh. Families of deer came to the pond. I inherited two Moscovi ducks from the farmer down the lane, all white with bright red-orange beaks and feet. I called them St. Michael and Gabriel, and before long, could tell the difference between the two of them. My Labrador, Rodin, even moderated his idea of sport in chasing them, and they became an expected part of the landscape as trees took on leaf and color, and daffodils and crocus and a blue flower rampant as clover covered the land.

There was a standing arrangement with the farmer one field over to harvest the hay on my farm for his animals, and he would periodically drive over in his red pickup to check the prospects of the summer's bounty. His son could chop a cord of firewood and stack it in two hours. I hired the son for that, and sometimes the father and the grandkids came to fish at my pond. It's about all the human company I had, but I'd known what I was in for and at the time, wanted it.

The brutality of the winter was over. We'd survived the endless storms and weeks without electricity, and water, and phones. The trees had been so covered in ice so often that their branches would drop, invariably on the road leading out, from the weight. At least fifteen entire trees went down that way. I got more expert at using a chain saw, and who to call for the jobs I couldn't handle. I also got blisters and aching muscles, rampant poison ivy, scrapes and bruises and a serious cut or two, and a hell of a lot stronger. I would find myself standing on the porch, girding my loins for whatever lay ahead and then marching into it, armed with my axe. After a bad flood, my small bridge at the curve in the road to the barn washed out. It needed shoring up with logs and boulders. It turned into a sizeable two-day project, but I couldn't drive out until it was done. Every day was like that. Something to attend to that was tied to basic survival, and it made a changed person of me. There was no way to put things off. There was, most of the time, no way to get help. So you did it, immediately, and the best you could. The triumph of achievement was enormous, although I stopped congratulating myself so often or beaming with pride as the chores grew in number and came as less of a surprise and it was just forward ho. I sure admired the wild animals more for their struggles, and willing attitude toward taking on anything that came their way.

❖   ❖   ❖

Vixen showed no interest, and simply bypassed the tiny kitten who'd died at the tunnel entrance, and I decided it was time to bury it, deep enough outside to keep it undisturbed. The wild animals all around us were so unused to the presence of humans on their acres, that they ignored my arrival. Except for Rodin and his bark and bite, we probably would have seen even more.

The fox were red tailed and nearly as large as a small dog. There were raccoons, which did come out at night and did try at garbage pails, and did get chased by Rodin. There were bobcats and bears. And the Blue Ridge range was a migratory trail for birds of considerable size. There were landmarks I'd already seen where birdwatchers, serious in their pursuits with telescopes and reference books and note taking, gathered to record the flight

73

patterns and number. I found out that eagles and other large raptors keep close to the tops of the mountains to make rest stops. The forest I lived in was full of incredible silent owls. There were bountiful hawks. There were, in essence, a lot of big things that ate small things. It was against these predators that the clever Vixen was protecting herself and her brood.

❖   ❖   ❖

The brilliance of cats in such matters was not new to me. I witnessed it first with Brownie Golden Swallow (named half after her tortoiseshell coloring and half after a female Chinese Kung Fu movie star), who hid her first litter in the unfinished ceiling of the old New York brownstone we once lived in. She would leap from the sink, into a space in the broken tin ceiling, and had made a nest somewhere inside the rafters. It was the dogs a hallway and room away that motivated her, not her lack of trust in me. When I realized what she'd done, I made her a proper home in a large covered box on the bathroom floor, instructed her to bring every single kitten down to it, and one at a time, she did. But we had two years of adoration between us at the time. To Vixen, I was a stranger and had all the strangeness of a human, and she wasn't falling for any of it.

The days were warming up. The feedings were going well. I found that Vixen would allow me to situate myself halfway up the staircase to the loft and watch her and the babies feed below. I started looking around up there, and mostly it was sealed boxes of the owner's previous life. But I found one near the top of the stairs, packed with rag rugs, and a larger rug rolled halfway over the top and signs of a cat that'd been spending time in it! Could Vixen have been vacationing up there? She was so protective, so tightly wound up about the safety of the children, I thought not. That meant another cat, one I'd not yet met. So I started putting food up there, too, and that food started disappearing overnight.

About a week of this had gone by and I returned to my perch to watch the family at their meal, and walked right in on a magnificently huge, deep orange male cat, the kind with enormous important jowls that would win trophies, who was drinking away at the bowl of rich evaporated milk without a care for whether I was on his turf or not. I started to talk to him, and I petted him and he put up with all of it, and purred.

For every bit that Vixen didn't trust me, this boy was filled with faith. I sat next to him. He came to me and sat in my lap. I called him Foxfire.

Because my trips to the barn were no longer a gauntlet run through miserable weather, but a delightful path through wild roses and ferns, a calmer stream, and the sun shining on all, I made several off-schedule arrivals a day, and sometimes even in the dark of the warm southeast summer nights. I could now see that Foxfire joined in the family grooming, eating, and visiting.

❖   ❖   ❖

Before May, the entire Vixen and Foxfire family was eating on it's own, present and accounted for at every breakfast. There were six kittens in all. Vanguardinia and her little brother who matched and I named Wolfie because of his appetite, would run if I tried to pet them, but got used to my trying and growled through every bite, but it was all talk. The others would scurry back into the tunnel, peering out, crying pitifully for the discomfort of what to do. Vixen continued to send mixed signals. I got to see all the flurry of them, but not in detail so I could tell them apart. All were orange and white but for one tortoiseshell. I named her Golden Swallow II, after my New York Brownie. She stayed elusive.

Rodin and springtime were madly in love. He'd take off early, run the fields and forests, return wet, and brambly, and grinning ear to ear for chow, then off again. He gave all the local deer and fox a run for their money. I tried to contain him, or chain or hold him to a tree on a hundred foot clothesline, but he broke every bind, and I was afraid if it broke at the tree and not the collar, he'd get wound around something and trapped, too far away for me to know he was in trouble. So I gave up, and in return for my retirement of restriction, he started to come when I whistled, or when I turned over the engine on the car.

The cats knew exactly when Rodin was out on a run. One morning, in a sight which I was totally unprepared to see, which touched me deeply and to tears, I was met on my way to the barn by Vixen, and a screaming Vanguardinia and Wolfie. Vanguardinia made the most fiercesome face like an oriental temple dog. I don't know if she was imagining that she had to do me in to get the bounty, or if it was the mix of terror and joy Vixen had taught them all. I got to putting down the tray for this new routine, repeated every morning from then on, so they could tear into it first. When they calmed down, I was allowed to bring what was left into the barn for the other less brave kidlets and exceedingly patient dad.

Vixen never did more that tolerate me, as it turned out. She was angry all the time. I tried to pet her once, and she raked the back of my hand for my trouble, then stared me down, hissing, and when she knew she'd gotten me in line, continued eating.

I kept the bowl filled with a pound or more of dry food, a dog water dish filled with milk, and a huge water bowl as well as the twice a day canned food feeds. The plates were always empty by the time I made my rounds. In late May, some sense of regularity settled in. I didn't want to draw any other creatures into the barn or near the babies, so I started cutting back and we worked out the volume required for six kits and two grownups. I still fed Foxfire at the top of the loft steps near his bed, and I don't think anyone else ever fed there. Protocol.

One morning, I found one of the little ones who'd remained a stranger to me, outside the barn. There was no way to tell what had gone wrong, no wounds, but it appeared to have simply stopped living. I buried the baby and mourned with Vixen, who accepted these things far better than I did. Cats, and probably most animals, seem to know something about the cycle of life more than we do. I wondered if in spite of death, they maybe never stop seeing and knowing each other on some other level, because they grieve, but not in the same way.

Vanguardinia was my favorite, because she spoke so directly and with such intensity to me, though I am ashamed to say

She spoke so directly and with such intensity to me...

I never knew her exact meaning. She still would not let me near her, so, like her brother Wolfie, also a favorite and a touch more trusting, I admired them from afar. The others were still mad dash out and back, and when the tunnel entrance no longer accommodated the stouter Vixen or growing kittens, they hid til I left in their new places around the barn. You can't keep a good cat down.

❖   ❖   ❖

We got hit with a surprise storm, the temperature suddenly dropping and snow flying through the air long after I was sure we'd seen the last of it. It was then, that Foxfire vanished. Every day I checked, but there was no sign of his having been in the bed he'd made in the loft box. I put pieces of straw or oddly folded the rug so I'd know if it had been moved, but the next day, it was as I left it. I'd seen the interplay between Foxfire and Vixen and the babies. He was a protective mate and father, and he'd never have left them willingly. Sometimes he'd lie down next to Vixen when she nursed, watching them, cleaning an ear or a leg. He was remarkable and rare. I thought them all deeply in love and dependent on each other.

Vixen never revealed much to me, and that included little reaction to Foxfire's absence. But I pictured her at night on the widow's walk of the loft's edge, waiting and looking and hoping. Foxfire was a huge specimen of a cat, sturdy and in fine fettle, as they all were. I didn't think he could fit in the tunnel or had hidden in there. He'd shown no signs of illness at all.

The fourth day of not finding Foxfire, I'd already been through the woods, walking the hills, carrying an open can of odiferous tuna, calling out and grief-stricken for myself and the family he'd raised. I took Rodin on a leash, saying, "Find Foxfire, Ro, where's the big cat. Find Foxfire," and he looked and smelled and pulled for it, but we did not see him. A sickly animal in the wilds, if that had happened, was something that didn't happen, because they just don't make it.

I figured Foxfire was accustomed, like Vixen, to thwarting the enemy. I did not know why he would have gone missing. It saddened the whole tenor of what, day after day for months had been the successful survival of all but two. I witnessed the prettiness of it as they grew and prospered, and had constant discovery in their ways. We'd been through the worst part, the infancies and the winter. It couldn't possibly come to a bad end.

Anyone who has ever fed an animal, wild or domestic, and then had the connection severed by surprise will know how I felt. I had horrific imaginings. Like the first time I let my city girl, Babette, out on a mountain lawn to explore, hovering over her like an idiot, sure an eagle would swoop down and grab her. In spite of me, Babette taught herself how to climb trees, walk on a grape trellis and bask in the sun and breeze. She trained me to leave her alone, and was very kind to return to the house when I got ridiculously desperate.

Foxfire was a different story. For one thing, I wasn't sure exactly what day I'd noticed he'd gone or his food dish remained full. I didn't pay attention right away; I thought it a one-night aberration. We'd had a very cold week. I heard the owl cry at night more than usual. I'd seen a fox at the pond, which later killed and dragged off one of my beautiful ducks, Gabriel. After that, St. Michael slept in the water or at the edge of the rickety dock. I made a floating thing for him, clumsy but useful, that I anchored mid-pond. But Foxfire stayed missing, and I thought the worst.

Vanguardinia was the unexpected link and comfort. She was fearless, and held her own opinions about me. Vixen was satisfied to wait for me in the barn now, with food to be counted on, and doing a superb job of raising her family. But little Vanguardinia, who now sported a lovely array of broad orange stripes on a white ground and diamond on her brow and white toes, came every morning, halfway to the porch of the log cabin, to lead me to the family lest I forget my duty. She let me pet her now. She got ham and chicken for her early visits whenever I had it, and we came to spend her feeding time on the path, sitting next to a small brook that passed through the property, banked by unfurling ferns and bearded purple iris. She was very dear to me. She helped me over the missing of the one other family member I'd been close to, her poppa. Vanguardinia had her mother's ferocity, but she'd absorbed her father's trust, and I was grateful. There was still nothing to show that Foxfire had returned to his bed or his dishes. At the end of two weeks, I stopped putting his meals up in the loft.

❖   ❖   ❖

You would hear the screams of animals in the woods at night sometimes. I admired them all, predator and prey, and wanted them all to live. I wouldn't want an eagle to die of starvation. I'd watched the miracle of silent flight of a massive screech owl at night once, on a moonlit walk with Rodin. Their wingspan is huge past believing. I never knew who I should root for, the same experience I have watching nature films. I just didn't want any harm to come to the ones who had turned into personal friends.

❖   ❖   ❖

In my log cabin and beside a cozy fire with a good meal in me and a nice glass of cognac backed with coffee, I was missing a book on Van Gogh's life I particularly wanted to read. It was my much dog-eared copy of his letters to his brother Theo, that I'd had since high school. I knew I had it somewhere, but clearly not in the house. After a good look around, I headed to the barn with a flashlight.

I found Vixen grooming herself on the little wooden platform that covered her tunnel. They were all very sanguine now. I'd fed them a few hours before; there was no noisy panicked departure. Vanguardinia came to me to say hello and Vixen no longer protested her enthusiasm. I set about to open an unpacked box of my books, trying to find Van Gogh.

There was a noise above me in the loft. I shone the light to the top step and beyond, and it flashed against the bright and beautiful and desperately longed-for vision of Foxfire. He had come home.

As I raced up the staircase, he backed into shadow, my first indication that something was wrong. It was out of character, because we liked each other. He stood looking at me, and his leg collapsed under him. I didn't want to shine the light in his face any more than I'd want it in mine, but it was pitch dark inside, and I had to see and touch him. Since I never made a trip to the barn without a can of food in my pocket, I pulled it out and opened it and spilled it in front of him on the planks. He moved forward as best he could, off balance, unable to stand, and he ate. He shuddered when I touched him. He gulped the food ravenously. He was thin, and he was injured. I moved my hand lightly along his body, which he let me do, and I found the horrifying thing his leg had become. I don't know the real name, but the extroverted knee of the cat's back leg, now ended at the joint. What wavered below was an atrophied stump, and no foot, no paw. The hair had almost gone from visible bone. I brought my hand quickly over my mouth to keep from screaming out. There was a huge gash at his hamstring, but healing had started. There was no puffiness of infection, and no blood on the area. I could not imagine the pain he'd endured, crippled this way, what the trip back home, and up the staircase to familiar safety, had cost him. I sat next to Foxfire stroking him and talking to him and gently urged his body sideways onto my lap, which he permitted. I had the feeling he had returned minutes before I arrived, and that maybe turning on all the porch lights late at night, and the flashlight, and had I whistled or sang on the path? Well, maybe it was all the beacon that led him those last yards back to us. Vanguardinia, silent for the first time since I met her, had come to join her dad and me, and was standing in front of Foxfire. After a minute, she began tentative licking at his ears and face. Vixen came upstairs and lay next to him. The flashlight was up-ended a few feet away casting a yellow light around us. I wept shamelessly in front of the whole brave family.

We comforted each other in the homecoming for a long time. He let me place him on his familiar blanket, and fell into a deep sleep, which I could not do myself for many hours more.

Back on my own bed, I tried to imagine what had happened. I thought he'd hurt himself getting extricated from a trap or the trap of another animal after him. A beak, teeth, claws?

In the days and weeks that followed, the atrophied lower bone fell off, and he taught himself to balance without it, negotiating the stairs and barn planks almost as well as if it had never happened. But he was in a spot now, not swift anymore and therefore not safe. It changed the chances for the survival for all of them, and I wasn't sure about the altered state.

Of course I wanted to bring them all inside my cabin. Of course I wanted them forever in my life and household. There were a lot of problems to solve with that, too.

I figured I could get Foxfire to let me introduce him to a cat carrier, but was not sure I could get him inside it, or what damage he might further do himself at the fury of being held captive. He wasn't used to it.

❖　　　　❖　　　　❖

I've spent a good many years of my life rescuing animals in trouble, and there are things you can wickedly trick them into and still feel virtuous. But I have noticed in the past decade or so in America, an absolute frenzy to capture and castrate cats and dogs. I believe in limited populations, but you can accomplish that by segregating the boys from the girls without destroying their virility. It takes a little more effort, walls hastily built from two by fours and chicken wire and a bigger apartment every time you move. But I never thought cutting off somebody's balls a casual thing. Most city dwellers share their lives with sterile animals. It is more rare than not to see the birth and continuing community of cat or dog families. To have the chance to see this intact family, growing and caring for each other before my eyes, and in arrangements made to suit their feral appetites, was something I did not know if I'd see again. As a matter of fact, I haven't.

Given the passion for it in our times, castration would be the veterinarian's first priority. I didn't know any local vets, not just well, but not at all. There were crusaders with good intentions to watch out for too, who made careers of these things. I would have to give my name and location, it would be on the paperwork and check I'd pay with (that might bounce) and eventually the whole story would tumble out. There were probably more males in Vixen's litter, like Wolfie. That alone would start a dervish around their future ability to procreate, which might in no time be out of my control. Or I might come up against a stone wall on Foxfire's survival at all, for there are many who think infirmities require no remedy short of death.

This had been a great astounding privilege to know these cats. Nature had already mysteriously eliminated two of the litter, and by selection and disaster, more might die before the year was out.

Very little in the world is quite as beautiful as a cat. I was seeing them wild, at their best. A friend happily described the cat to me as the original all terrain vehicle. And their bravery was beyond and out of proportion to most people. They don't whimper, or fuss, or complain except under the most extreme duress. What kind of betrayal would be in store for the father of a family who risked his life and limb to return, whether to continue his patriarchy, or just see them one last time. And to lessen his chance of survival, now even rougher with part of his leg gone, by castrating him? Male cats are less aggressive, and lose their odor after castration. One of his own kind might fight him for his position, the sense of the male gone. Could I find a vet within a hundred miles to knowingly return an un-castrated cat to the wilds? It was all too unfair.

❖   ❖   ❖

Foxfire's wound had healed, and the stub was useful to some degree. We were nearing the end of the summer. One more of the kittens had vanished from the daily count and I never found it. Predictably, the family was growing smaller, but they were together, loving each other. Vanguardinia and Wolfie had become most special to me.

There had been, only briefly, the consideration of bringing them all in, individually or otherwise, into the log cabin's life and domesticating them. I had my own cats inside. There wasn't enough room to give the barn family their own room, which they would require, as they were fighters.

❖   ❖   ❖

The months passed on. The summer was lush and florid. The days long and warm. Vixen and Foxfire's family no longer depended on the food I provided. We'd cut way back, though I still left cat kibble and milk and water in the barn, and the dishes were not emptied out and licked clean like before. Vixen had taught her youngsters how to catch their own meals, which I'm sure she thought superior food, or at the very least, wise. She never changed her opinion of me, though we both knew the vittles I brought her that winter strengthened her and helped the babies. The unforgettable images of her nurturing were far and away enough to reward me. My intrusion on their privacy had been useful to them, but that usefulness was drawing to a close. I had wonderful sketches and photographs of the summer and them in it. Somewhere in all of us, we would not forget each other as long as we lived.

Vanguardinia and Wolfie were no longer the constant duo. Vanguardinia would sometimes risk sitting out a sunset on my lap on the porch, alert to every sound and impending disaster between catnaps. She purred, as had her father, Foxfire, when I petted. October was on its way. November, my lease was up.

The family of farmers who'd come for the hay harvesting, had seen the cats in the barn, and I arranged for them to care for them during the next winter, and if they thought it possible, to bring them to their farm. I left a good Savage Over and Under rifle/shotgun with them, and got a promise that they'd keep an eye on the family of Vixen and Foxfire, in exchange. One of the farmer's children, locally renowned for duck catching, was going to get St., Michael back to their pond in a week.

I decided to kidnap Vanguardinia. I started leaving a large open cat carrier on the porch, and put treats for her closer and closer to the door. But she suspected something was up, and refused to visit me again for three days straight. She called all the shots, as always. She took the initiative to leap into my lap. I was not allowed to pick her up. And any holding too tightly of this fierce little person was met with hissing and biting. I knew she loved me as much as I loved her, and didn't mind the reaction that sometimes left me bleeding. It seemed perfectly sensible to me, and anyway, my motives were bad. What had I to offer this little girl? I didn't know what lay ahead for me, and my Labrador Rodin, and any of my indoor cats. We were still on the move, trying new territory, and probably heading south and then most likely, west. Vanguardinia had her mother's surety of survival. She was also an intrinsic part of the family. She loved Vixen with all her heart; I'd seen it when they were together. Except for her times with me, they were inseparable. And she had become her father's keeper, grooming him and making sure he had food, which he allowed and relished from her. It's true, I watched her make her way up the loft steps once with a piece of ham in her teeth, and drop it in front of him. They were a rare family.

❖   ❖   ❖

The day the moving van came, all the cats disappeared. I hoped the roar of the trucks and activity and unaccustomed voices of strangers had driven them only temporarily from their barn. I had made the time the week before to say our goodbyes, and tried to explain leaving them which I couldn't fully understand myself. For many decades, I'd made a home for any animal I ever found.

In my last look back, I spotted Vanguardinia sitting on top of the tractor, watching me. I leapt from my car to run to her. But in the space it took, she'd gone. She'd finished with me, as had Foxfire, and Vixen, and Wolfie, and the two others I never got to know. Proving her mother's caution right, that humans are, after all, transient and feckless.

VI

The Gandy Dancer

The Gandy Dancer

The payoff for the job was the miles of colored satin fripped by the hilltop wind. And the night fog-split skies. And, inevitably, singular human contact.

Otherwise, working the weddings at the California horse ranch would have been boring, and it was not. It all took place on a twelve hundred acre estate, bought with dot com money by a couple of high rollers. There were horses to hire, horses to breed, horses to board, and the big house was rented out for weddings and fancy do's. The crowd hit in April, and petered out by September.

Despite the exclusive real estate, we were under the thumb of local ordinance and had to stop the live bands by nine pm. Our own rules forbid caterers or florists or wine merchants from showing any earlier than ten am. In between, lay the unknown.

It was not a bad job, keeping hostilities down between families, the children out of the koi ponds, the photographers out of the private gardens, and the musicians plugged into sockets that worked. Assuring the occasional bride that the pregnancy didn't show was covered by the bridesmaids.

It was around midnight that the last guest was ushered into limos, and unless they'd made an early retreat, that the bride was changed for the honeymoon. I'd usually find the mom alone in the little bride's suite where her daughter had strewn and forgotten remnants which, for the very last time, she'd be picking up after her child. Flowers and plants would get divided up, shoes and cell phones found, and the only thing left would be turning out the lights and closing the gate. A generous party would leave leftovers for the underpaid staff. I got the bottom two tiers of the wedding cake once. The moods were generally good, and the days theatrical. Keeping two hundred and fifty guests in line, happy, and from exploding anything was a challenge we met.

❖   ❖   ❖

This particular day, the standard assortment of what could go wrong, was. The parking attendant hadn't shown up. Bees, the yellowjacket kind, were getting into the salmon and sauces and the caterers wanted to set up inside somewhere. The pet goat wandered into the dining courtyard uninvited, and was being pursued unsuccessfully by waiters in tuxedo shirts, flailing linen napkins. The goat, whose name was Kumbayyah, was the only emergency that showed promise of being handled. His favorite cowpuncher, Katy, could get him to do anything. I ran to the office to call her.

Kumbayyah got handled. Meanwhile the musicians were getting drunk and petulant. They'd been flown in for the weekend by the groom's buddies, from New Orleans. They were coked up, fancied themselves the Rolling Stones, and they didn't approve of the venue. I found the best man, ascertained that he was footing their bill, and suggested he use a little muscle. Whatever he did, it worked.

Inside one of the pretty inner courtyards of this old Spanish style estate, bridesmaids had become flying yards of crimson satin and chiffon, racing corner to corner like temple kites, in search of the box of wrist corsages. The wedding coordinator was burning up cell phone minutes, florists were unleashing gorgeous flowers on every surface, the bride's youngest brother was in a corner regurgitating beer, and one of the ranch hands said a water main had broken, but it didn't look like it would effect the big house. Which was good news, as no water added problems I don't even want to remember or describe.

By now, the wife of the couple who owned the ranch was uncorking some primo California wine and headed for her teepee to forget the crowd, ever growing, and the prospects for the antiques she'd filled the place with over decades of collecting. The ten thousand dollar, one-day fee compensated for a lot of grief. I found her going into hiding, to announce that the photographer had tromped the entire wedding party into her private garden. It was rule number one on the list: DON'T let them do it. Today, she didn't care. It was part of the treachery for us managers, the rules changing at whim.

I continued to the main lawn and gazebo, to make sure all the seats that had been ordered were set up, and I checked my clipboard charts. The redwood benches were drying fast from the morning's hosing, and were laced with garlands of white and crimson roses, lilac satin woven through them. Someone in an exquisite violet gown was checking the microphone. The bride's sister, I thought, remembering her from a rehearsal. She was a professional singer, and was going to acappella an operetta. The sound system was working.

The setting on the formal grass hilltop was without compare. The soft rolling mountain range in the distance was taking on a muted blue, the higher points hit with sunny gold. A vineyard ran down the hill for acres, bordered by red roses in full bloom. Every now and then silver clouds of dust, the sun caught in them, would let fly as either a single or dozen horses stirred a thick trail through the pasture beyond. I'd always take the time to watch them rear up, feign threats to each other, then take off at a gallop.

Across a curved wooden bridge, white calla lilies, white and orange tiger lilies, lilac clusters, white fragrant freesia, and dozens more I didn't know the names for were tied to railings, caught up in vases, and trailing from tree branches. It was a divine blow of perfumed air, and carefully executed by the firm hired to pull it off. The staffs were pure pro. They outdid each other through the season. We rarely had incompetents, except if an extra was hired blind, and drank his way through the day or made too much noise. Small wars might break out between competing forces, but didn't last. Reputations counted big, and it was a small world.

The only place I hadn't checked out yet was the nursery, provided for underaged children of the guests. We supplied the nannies. I was surprised to find the room closed and empty. Apparently no babies this day. The nursery was a sweet if pretentious room filled with children's furniture, costly stuffed animals, and games and a VCR, a day bed, crib, a couple of rocking horses and rocking chairs, and a small kitchen and bathroom. It doubled as a changing room for staff or the band. We kept the door padlocked to eliminate the chance of walking in on guests having sex, carried away with the hormone ripe day.

I continued my patrol. In one of the smaller courtyards, I spotted a terribly thin elderly man, resting on the edge of a brick planter. A younger man, who turned out to be his son, was next to him.

The son's face was down with concern. But he had the puffed up proud posture, touched with cold fear, that identified him at once as the father of the bride. I introduced myself, and asked if I could be of service.

In the course of the greeting, we all shook hands. I liked them both immediately, moreso the world-weary thin, and possibly sickly fellow, called Pop. His bright eyes betrayed any intention the rest of his body had in hurtling him toward the grave.

I would have put him in the neighborhood of ninety, and liked the strength of his hands, and found myself intrigued by that lined face and the wellspring of his old Irish soul that danced in his flirtatious blue eyes. I asked if I might make him a cup of tea.

"I think he'd like that, would you, Pop?" his son said.

"I would now yes, I would fancy a good cup, if its no trouble t'ye."

"Not in the least," and I offered him a crooked elbow. His son and I got Pop to his feet.

"We have a private room that's not being used." I pointed across the courtyard to the nursery. "It's warm, and when the sun goes down, he'll need it. And there's a day bed. I can make his tea in the kitchen."

"Would you like that, Pop?"

The son was on one side of the sweet old guy, and I was on the other. He was a little shaky on his pins. Pop must've been a long drink of water in his younger days. He towered over me, and wasn't fully upright. He could walk okay, but slow.

The bride's father, the son of this man, was nervously looking around, so I nodded him off, that I had the situation under control. He seemed to be wanting to take charge like a general would, seeing the troops gone awry, but had, like most of the fathers of the brides, been excluded. Probably a man who ran a large corporation, and not liking this reduction to just paying the bill. Apparently, being told to have fun wasn't necessarily pleasant if you're not accustomed to it.

"Thanks," the son said to me. "He's having a rough day. Lots going on, isn't there. I'm not so good at standing aside!" He laughed, and looked for a direction in which to head. I told him to check on his dad whenever the impulse struck, and I led Pop to the nursery.

❖   ❖   ❖

Pop put up a fight over my wanting to get him stretched out on the bed with his shoes off, and a light blanket over him. But finally, he did lay down, and shoes still on, accepted the blanket. I heard him give out with a sigh when I turned on the stove, grabbed up the tea kettle, filled it and set it to boil.

"I can't remember why I'm here," Pop said. "That was my son. You met my son. We were at his house all day, they picked me up and we drove here last night. I had a drink before we left but it was only one, and I can't say when I got so hard hit by liquor as that! I been throwin' up, and don't know why. It's a party, isn't it, though I can't get it straight. I don't know the people here for sure. I don't know them."

The bride was his granddaughter. He'd been living in Texas, and she'd been in school in Europe, and although they hadn't seen much of each other, she'd included him in on her big day.

Pop closed his eyes, and the kettle whistled. I asked if he liked the tea bag right in there or waved briefly over the cup or what. I'm a coffee drinker, which requires no ritual. He wanted it in, to steep, "Of course!" and then a spoon with which to fish it out. I helped him sit, and propped him upright with pillows.

"My Betty's not here. This is the first time I've gone anywhere without her. I guess I can't stand it. Not that I thought I could. You make a good cup of tea."

I pulled up the nanny rocker to the side of the narrow bed. Pop was looking a little more solid. Color in his cheeks, but his eyes were watering. I put a box of Kleenex next to him.

93

"I should go out," he said. "D'ya think I should go back out? I feel as if I'm lettin' them all down. What is it that's going on?"

"It's a wedding, and you're a guest. Your son knows you're here, and he's pleased that you're comfortable. Don't worry."

Pop blew his nose.

If he couldn't remember the granddaughter or that she was the bride, I didn't want to add to his embarrassment, although there wasn't a drop of need for it. The emotion of these days doesn't get covered up for long. It's a complex, layered thing, a lot of memories and regret and sadness come with it. Pop was just the first and too old to hide what he felt.

"Oh," he said simply, "young people," as if to purge his guilt. "Not that I'm not used to a crowd, or youngsters, mind ye." He finished his cup. "I was eleven of twelve kids. Or maybe I was seventh? We lived in New York. We lived upstate."

I brought him a fresh cup of tea, and took the first one back to the sink.

"Too big a crowd at home," Pop said, "So damn many, and not enough to eat, and then me father died. It were a rough time. We managed, warn't pitiful n' that. Fore long, up comes me father's brother, my uncle, he were, and he stands in fer us, and marries me widowed mum. Not uncommon neither, in them days. Didn't like him, though. I run off."

I was settled back in prime location. His voice was as slight and gentle as the storyteller. Not weak, not rasping, but melodic like a lullaby. The voice of a singer. And he began to tell me about his youth, and a time that maybe filled him with as much joy as anything since. His face was animated by what he spoke.

"I rode the rails! I was fourteen, and off I walked, right from home to the rail yards and hopped me a freight. It was full, too. All them cars and hobos hangin' off ladders and flat out on rooftops of them cars, and inside, too, if they could get in, freights loaded down with goods. Ye had t'hide from the watchmen. I seen some, mean as piss, take an' throw a lad from a fast mover onto a cinder bed, down the hills or off the bridges, they didn't care, one less bum."

Pop shifted back, then looked up and the irreverent brightness of a deed ill done, but done none the less, burst from him.

"Jesus we was free! So free! The sky at night, packed up with stars, the dawn, and the coming into a city. I'd drop off at a slow, and head for a farmhouse maybe, and maybe catch some work and maybe catch some hell. Ye took the chance of it. If ye got lucky and could farm chore? Then there was that, and a bed, regular like. Home cooked meals of quality…but say, you didn't like the food? Nor boss? Nor a cross-eyed look? And off ye went. Sometimes there'd be the luxury of drink and a smoke. But always, it'd get to be a bore, and back then on the rails, ridin' the rails."

❖   ❖   ❖

By now, the wedding party on the other side of the door had become a far-removed thing. I was lost to America in the Depression, and a tall lanky rider of the rails, making his way across it. There was an old brass light fixture on the side of the nursery entrance and it was the only light we could see each other's faces by as the day was graying outside the window. But I was inside some trainman's shack, next to steel tracks trembling with power, locomotives in and out of the yards, pipe and kerosene smoke clouding the air.

"I went down deep in Texas, way down, through the state, can't recall towns by name so good. Got nabbed by the track guard. They pulled us all out, and he says, the state of Texas wants ye to dig holes, and he points to the ground. Here, he says, and there, and then here, and he shows us. And we get a shovel and dig. Then we get marched to a farmhouse and they feed us good, damn I can remember that! Texas believes in food. Never seen the like of it anywhere else. Then we gets herded back and shovels some more, and there's guards, and with shotguns, too. That's the way it went. Shows us where he wants the holes dug for Texas, and that we do. After a couple of weeks, we'd got the fine paid off, from illegal riding the rails. It was a good life."

Pop got up to use the bathroom and didn't want more tea. I put the cups in the sink. There was no need to turn on more lights, and when he came out, he pulled up a second nanny rocker near mine, and sat quietly. He interested me greatly, and I wondered if the granddaughter bride had ever been treated to the old man's history, and that the greatest shame of being young was how little interests you beyond yourself.

"Then," Pop picked up on the moment of liberation, "the last day of all the holes dug for Texas, the man squares us up in a line, and marches down it and give us fifty cent each one, and he says, 'Now this here fine Union Pacific Railroad which you has taken advantage of, but paid your debt to make it right, has got no more hold on you, and that's the law, you're free to go,' says he, 'but you got far more trouble,' he puffs up to say it loud then, 'far more trouble worse'n this yer in we catch ya twice! So what'll it be with the lot o'ya,' he wants to know. 'Ya leaves by foot, which is fine, or I got three open rail jobs, which yer lucky t'have laid at yer feet,' says he, 'and that,' says he, 'is the choices, boys. So what'll it be? Ya paid yer debt all round.'"

Pop was laughing at the memory, and wiped his grinning eyes with the fragile, unworkmanlike fingers he had now, and continued.

"So me, the youngest and the dumbest, I'm still standing there with my mouth open and all the rest is gone fast. So I looks at the boss and I says, what it come to, this rail work? And how's it pay?" Pop sat forward and put his hands on his hips. " 'Where you from, boy?' says the boss, 'that y'don't know the work of the Gandy Dancer?' And I says New York, and he was that sorry for me, and says I should be thankful I stayed over this while in Texas. The pay was a quarter a day or summat like that. Maybe a nickel every fifty mile or so. Dangerous work, too, which I come to know but not from his mouth! He makes it out like pie and ice cream, a job for lazy boys, and no it warn't. So I tried it. Then after I broke me arm, I guv it up, and rode the rails again, back to New York after all, and Texas behind me."

"Then you settled in New York?"

He looked shocked. "Settled? Nay, settle's not fer me! I saw me sister in New York though, and tried to stay with her a bit.

She'd got married and she'd got a whole gang o'kids already, and she says stay, but will I work on the farm she'll feed me and I'll have a bed. I did a bit, but then I didn't like her much, and I didn't like her old man even less. The house was small, and jammed with so many and in a mess. Isn't it funny? A campfire and trail's got a neater look to it than no good folks in a little house." Pop took a breather.

"So, I hopped the rails and went back to Texas, and did some Gandy dancin' as I'd done, then guv it up when I met Betty." There was a soft sigh and a smile when he used her name. "I was seventeen. I could get regular work, but it warn't to my liking. My heart still turns over at the sight of a train, I'll tell you that, and that's the truth. But women, they get you to do things you never had in mind for yourself to do, and then we had little ones on the way. Betty and me, we was seventy years together, a month short of seventy-one and she's left me. Two months ago, she says to me, 'My journey's done, and I love you,' and then she died. Now this here suit?" Pop was wiping at his eyes and looked a little annoyed at himself. He can't have known the effect on me, or maybe seen I was redeyed, too. "This suit's the first time I had it on since her funeral. She was beautiful, my Betty. And she was my friend. But the woman never understood how I loved the trains."

❖   ❖   ❖

Pop's son came into the room to see how things were going. He looked calmer. He said the ceremony had ended and they were sitting down to eat. He hated his dad's missing the good parts, but was worried about the strain on him. He told me, too, as the old man lay down again and closed his eyes, that when his mom had died, his Pop's Betty, it had kind of blown him away. They could hardly get Pop to eat. He'd lost nearly fifty pounds. But the son said it happened two years ago, going on two and a half. I told him we were doing fine. That his daughter probably needed him more.

"I don't know," said the son. "I don't think she does need me anymore."

"She does now, and she always will," I said. "Trust me. I've met the source of your family."

It's not usual to closet up with a guest. I went out while Pop slept, to see if I was being missed. Everything seemed okay, and the party atmosphere about normal and all the disasters had happened early. Staff reinforcements arrived at three, and there were enough of us wandering about. I went back into the nursery and pulled a second blanket over Pop's feet.

He had nodded off before I found out the details of the Gandy dancer's life, and I wasn't going to be cheated out of a full account. The words were familiar to me, but this was the closest I'd ever gotten to a railroad man. I made some noise at the sink in the hope of waking him up, gently. One of his grandkids came in with plates of food, one for me and one for Pop, a great thoughtfulness. The youngster said he didn't know how I could stand the old man's rambling, and left.

I set up a little folding table by the bed for our dinner, and Pop ate some, but not much. I encouraged him. I said that he'd get his strength back. But he looked at me in a hard way, and I could see on his face he didn't want anything back but his Betty.

"Okay, Pop, you have to tell me. What is a Gandy Dancer? I've heard the words and it's a wonderful image. I know it has to do with trains, but that's as far as I go."

"Well," he said, "it shouldn't surprise me, it's a trade past its time. But, basically, you work for the company, you work the rails, in a gang. Gandy, well that was the shovel maker. The people made the shovels! I worked for Union Pacific, and we laid track, going west. Always on the move, you sit at the open boxcar door, or lay down if you could get away with it. We wasn't watched 'til we come to a town, but you never knew where the company man would be coming from. Soon as not, the train stops, and up ahead a mile or so, there's a load of tie and rail, and you hops off and walks to it, and lays it back to the engine. Ties go atop the cinder, which some other crew is shoveled in. The rail goes cross it, and that's driven in. You don't want a gap as it derails a train, so you put your shovel under the rail, and the next guy shovels cinder and gravel under, and makes it sound. Ya jumped on it, see? To lift the ties, you danced on them Gandy Shovel Company shovels, see? Then back off and on again."

I could picture all of it, the hard work in the sun, the cold, or the rain, and little regard for anybody's comfort. The workers were probably young rough guys who came from all over the country for work, and glad to have a job that paid.

"I never got to know anybody well," Pop said, then tried another small mouthful. "Newcomers all the time, and some bringing word of your hometown, and maybe meeting up with somebody you knew. The engineers were hard men, a little full of themselves with driving these big locomotives. They could make hell for ya. And a good one, well they'd give you time at night by the stoker, out of the weather, though they'd put ye to work. Some'd give ye grub, and some'd make ye pay wages for it, out in the middle of nowhere, and some you'd want t'punch out, it'd make ye that mad. But if they knew ye by sight you was damn sure off the gang awhile, looking for a farmer's job. Somehow it always come up before pay day, so's broke y'd be again, and it's farm or motor fixin' on some ricky tractor."

❖   ❖   ❖

I could have gone a few more rounds with Pop. Sat there listening for a month. But the magic of nights like this was breathlessly short.

The first time it happened, it surprised me. The second time I was looking for it. Not one event ever passed without some phenomenal contact with another human being, words revealed I'd never heard said before, or said myself. Or an opportunity to fix something and make it right would turn into something monumental. Part of the reason was this fuel in the air, the rare occasion of friends and strangers brought together for one of the few remaining ceremonies in our times. Mankind's history was written in short bridges of one ceremony to the next, and now it's going away from us. Except for weddings and funerals and a handful of holidays, the tradition of ceremony is leaving the human experience.

Nights like this one with Pop were the only reason for me to keep the job, that stunning surprise of connection. There was way too much to put up with and the work was not so much challenging as exhausting at the day's end. It was maybe one of the oddest things to be employed doing. The wages were pathetic.

But there was no greed set on emotional content, and for that and for the scenery, there was no match. When you stood alone at the top of the hill at the end of the ranch lawn, you could see the road leading out. I watched the line of red taillights of the last cars with the guests, and slow moving ranch golf carts struggling back up the hill, headlights bouncing. The caterers were packing up their trucks, the florists retrieving glass vases and the musicians getting their amplifiers loaded into vans. Pop had been escorted to a car. We'd said goodbye.

The moon was full and lit the darkest places, even inside the shadows of the giant live oaks. There were a small group of waiters carrying dishes and folding up the umbrellas, and policing the lawns with flashlights for anything left behind. They stood out, bright white in their serving coats, laughing, and kidding around with each other. Sometimes you'd see the tentative hug of a budding romance. I usually pulled a couple of the crew onto the dark slope of the property so they could see the fog backlit by the moon. The whole of the Milky Way was overhead.

The caterers were wiped out, and the support system of this fabulous wedding was starting to unwind, bottoms-upping the leftover wine. The forced politeness and random petty bitchery was lifting off us all in a giddy steam. I was watching the movement around me and the stars above me and glad the day had come to an end.

"What did the bride's father do?" I asked one of the chefs. "He must've been pretty well fixed, to pull this off, I think we're looking at a million dollar weekend, the air fares and hotels and all this. Nice guy. What line of work is he in?"

"Railroads," the chef said to me. "I think he owns railroads."

VII

Edith's Story

Edith's Story

Edith's son had died. It happened in a traffic accident. He had hardly finished with youth, and had not touched manhood, and he was gone. And she didn't know.

Edith had been living on a small island in Maine. The winters were her beautiful solitude. She lived alone. By early spring, her canoe could weave the remaining ice to shore, and by arrangement with the town grocer, who nannied her year round, she'd make her first trek in to the dry snow-dotted earth of the mainland, to gather up the fresh supplies she'd ordered at Christmas.

❖   ❖   ❖

First stop was always the post office. Ralph was glad to see her and full of important gossip. As he filled her in, he brought out piles of letters and cards, magazines and packages, and stacked them in front of her at the window. One envelope stood out. It was a manila envelope, 9 x 12, and felt strange in her hands. It had a police department return address in the corner. But she dropped it with the rest into a canvas sack at her feet, which was neither large nor small in size or weight. Just a sack. But she could not forget the presence of the manila envelope, as if it held something burning.

The first week she always spent at Main-E-Ac's Bed & Breakfast. It was comfortable. Run by friends. She had the pick of any room, though she always ended up in the back corner suite, from which she could see her island home across the water and the town's twinkling night lights on the other side. It had a fireplace, and a beautiful quilt she loved on the old four-poster.

Edith ate breakfast with the family in their big downstairs kitchen. One child was off at school, one at the table with them, home all day every day, "driving us nuts," her father said, but kissed the little girl, and reminded her of the day's chores. Edith dropped her mail and knapsack in her room, and walked the three blocks to the garage, to pick up her car.

In every step and every view, she was reminded of how good it felt, this life she'd made for herself. The twenty years of life on her island, which nobody else had wanted and she'd bought for a song, and all the work of building her own house on it and raising her boy there. Good years, with all the usual troubles and all the usual joy. Edith was a musician, one of the few who'd made a decent living from it. Songs had paid for the life she loved. She whistled a passage from Puccini she'd been working on. As she walked, she started looking forward to driving again.

The old Land Rover had been hauled out front and the battery re-installed. It was an old one, about thirty years old, the rugged safari-looking kind, a dull army green with a spare tire fastened to the hood and a ladder up the back. Rachel was checking fluids and Larry considering the replacement of wires when she showed up, turning the corner by the gas pump and shouting out a greeting. She paid them for the winter's storage, a list of parts Larry had added, and congratulated them on Rachel's second pregnancy. Baby due by summer.

Edith got behind the wheel, and remembered how much she liked driving. She might return to Boston for a month and try spending some time with her son. She might not.

The size of Rachel's belly surprised her, the starting month's growth of a new child reminded her regretfully of the time passed since she'd seen or talked to her baby, the independent, grown, not-answering-letters, or noting the Christmas sweater baby.

She hadn't spoken to the boy in four months. He was asserting himself, angry, wanting to be alone, away from mom. And her life, maybe this spring especially was very different for Edith, too, than it had ever been before. She turned fifty this winter on her island. She found that nothing pressed on her. She felt her aloneness in the world, but was not lonely. But there was a shift, and she felt it keenly and didn't understand why.

❖   ❖   ❖

A day of errands brought Edith back to the B&B, after five, where she shared a glass of sherry with the family in their livingroom, and headed then up to her room. At six o'clock, a knock on the door would announce the arrival of the specially cooked dinner which she would eat alone in front of the fireplace, her armchair drawn up to a old round oak table, so common to the parts. The meal would be pan fried blue fish with lemon and butter and fennel, mashed potatoes in their skins, a rare steak and a salad. The dessert, which she could smell even now coming out of the oven, would be a cobbler of home canned peaches from last summer in bubbling brown sugar and the world's best crust. The fire had been started; she pulled her chair to it, and slid the phone across the table, to make room for the mail. All the things in view and touch had been prepared and tended by someone else, not her for once. The luxury of it, as always, descended over her.

Edith separated out and opened the manila envelope first, not knowing why she trembled. Knowing why she screamed. The crying without end had begun.

❖   ❖   ❖

I came to know these things about Edith much later, after we'd been friends for going on three years. I first met her in California. I'd just pulled off the side of the road to see the Pacific pounding the cliffs below Highway One. Edith was parked in her Land Rover against the side of a sand dune, in the front seat reading a book. She looked up and smiled. She was living in her car.

We saw each other again, a few weeks later, and sat down for coffee in a small Spanish café in Davenport, part of a beautiful surfer's haven south of San Francisco. This, then, is Edith's story.

❖   ❖   ❖

"I had a house once, no kidding, and I had an island under it! I really did," Edith told me, brushing crumbs off her shirt, running her fingers through her hair. "They were both small, it wasn't posh or anything, very rustic." She smiled. "Very, very rustic! No roads, so I had a canoe, a great green canoe." She looked away then back, to ask, "Ever try living like that? Takes a damn lot of work, that life."

I said I had, and watched the woman opposite me. I liked her. Edith was a reddish-brunette, with a sunburnt athlete's body. I took her for forty or 45 tops. She had a Russian-Mongol kind of face, cheekbones high that slid into a firm jaw and pointed chin. Her mouth was soft and full and her eyes a deep blue. I thought I could see her Maine waters in them. She turned out to be Irish and Jewish, half of each. I kept thinking something had beset her. Beset. Come down like a plague, sudden and terrible. She couldn't focus for long on anything. But as I said, I liked her.

Three months later we ran into each other again at a supermarket down the coast.

"I'm still camping out," Edith said to me. "I call it camping out. Sounds classier. How about you? Are you living here now? I guess I'm passing through. The jazz festival is coming up in Monterey. I might go. Maybe earn a few bucks, see some people. How do I reach you?"

Edith had been a Julliard student in New York and a violinist with the New York City Ballet Orchestra. She played a mean blue grass, and had several records to her credit, doing opera on two, and back up rock'n'roll on the rest.

We walked out into the parking lot loaded with groceries, and laughed at each of us still having the battered old cars we'd first seen each other in. Survivors.

When we shook hands to say goodbye, I felt something slipping away in her, and it scared me. I argued for it, and she gave in and followed me back to my place, for at least a meal and maybe to stay a few days.

I'd settled into a tiny bunkhouse on a ranch. We ate a big meal, and Edith lay down to sleep. She was there with me for three days, sleeping soundly through most of it. She ate, took showers, and visited the horses for part of the day, then read and slept. I had a waitress job: breakfast, lunch and home by four. On the third day, I came back and she had gone. I didn't see her again until November, four months later.

❖   ❖   ❖

Edith and I drove past each other on Carmel Valley Road and both of us slammed on the brakes, pulled over and ran into each other's arms, laughing like mad and hopping, so sure we'd never see each again. She had mailed me postcards from Montana, Utah, Nevada, the state of Washington and Puget Sound, and the last, from San Diego. I thought Mexico would be the next stop. I'd stayed put. She'd come back.

Edith had made some money playing what she called the sideshows, that is, not the main event but a good gig, nonetheless, and liked doing it. The vacant look to her was gone. She was robust. And wholesome, not the thread unwinding I'd always seen of her before. She'd been around for a week and was about to telephone me. She'd just rented a house on Laureles Grade, between Carmel Valley and Salinas. A home of her own again. That's where we headed. I'd finished work. The next day was Sunday, and the restaurant where I waitressed would be closed.

Edith and I ate a huge meal of steak and roasted vegetables and sweet corn, all grilled on a backyard pit. We drank scotch and walked through the sunflower filled meadow behind her house, watching the sun blow off the clouds and set behind purple-green hills in one of those goodbyes you never want to see end, that are finished in the blink of the eye, the color high and loud and deep as a Gregorian chant.

I had plenty of time, and was glad to be spending it with her. She made up the spare bed for me so I could stay the night. We got a fire going in the livingroom's old stone fireplace, and closed up the windows and doors against the cold, and talked about what we'd done and what was to come.

Edith took out her fiddle and played "Amazing Grace" with single notes that made us both cry. We had more scotch and threw on another log. And then she told me about the past five years she'd barely lived through, since that day she stepped on land, that spring in Maine.

❖   ❖   ❖

She'd just paddled in from her island and gone for her mail. There was a large manila envelope in it from the Boston Police Department. Her son had been killed in a traffic accident driving to an early morning job. By the time she found out, three months had passed. She hadn't seen him or talked to him for two months before that. And now he was dead. He'd been living in Boston, going to school, and wanted to be alone. Suited Edith, at the time, too. She'd had enough of children, even though he was her only child, and her cranky, demanding ex-husband, who kept trying to trump her in the parenting. The ex-husband knew where to find her, and how, but just hadn't wanted to. She never spoke to him again, and swore she never would.

"That was different, not talking to him," Edith said. "I couldn't talk to anybody, not at first. I had a lot of friends in Maine but I couldn't talk to any of them. I couldn't say 'My son is dead,' outloud. Then, all at once, the house and the island it was on seemed horrible to me. I'd always loved it. I'd been there almost twenty years and loved it then all at once, it seemed horrible and I couldn't get away fast enough. That damn manila envelope. I'll never..."

Edith filled our glasses and I got up for ice cubes. She was looking out the window over the meadow, dark as pitch except for a path from her kitchen lamp. Light traveled out to the tips of the sunflowers, like children in bonnets, all the same size and age.

"I did make one trip back, early next morning. But I didn't pack anything. I started throwing things away! Breaking things, lit the woodstove and burned things. I was setting fire to my previous life...so I stopped myself cold and paddled back to shore with one suitcase. I didn't know what I was doing. Acting out something."

"Where did you go? How on earth did you live?"

Light travelled
out ... the tips of
the sunflowers like
children in bonnets...

"Well, I guess I gave the keys to Rachel and Larry, they ran the garage in town and stored my car for me all winter. Good people. Rachel was three months from her second child. I didn't want to see that, either, I'll tell you. I didn't want to see anything. I told them to take the house and the island too. It was all paid for. I didn't ever want to see it again. I kind of, you know, lost it. I was non-functional in the extreme; I could hardly carry on a conversation. But I could drive, and drive I did. I gassed up the Land Rover and went to Minnesota. I had friends there, a family I'd been close to for years, from Julliard. They're both musicians, a piano and cello. They wanted me to stay. I couldn't even do that well. I was all adrenaline and movement. The way I'd felt on uppers to cram for a test at school, like that, but it was just me and my broken heart." Edith closed her eyes a minute, then suddenly said, "I want cake, want some cake? Here, say yes!"

Edith cut the cake, a triple layered chocolate thing that was terrific. I got more firewood from outside the back door and added three or four logs to the flames. I told her I wished I'd known, I wished I could have helped her in some way.

"You did."

"Edith, we hardly spoke, not about this, not about things of real content."

"I couldn't have," she said. "Not yet. But you helped. You treated that crazed woman you met like I was okay, and decent. And I am. But I had people asking me if I was on drugs, or lost my man. Jesus. I sure couldn't hold down a job."

Edith looked far away, outside the room in which we sat and beyond the mountains and the sky outside and maybe farther still into the stars.

"I drove to Los Alamos," she said. "I had it in mind to explode..." She laughed, deep and bitter. "And I lay down two days in the desert, just drove off the road, laid in the sand, took off all my clothes and roasted, froze at night, didn't drink water...I hoped actually coyotes would kill me."

"But you lived." I knew what that meant.

"Yes. I decided I must not have it in me to die, not then. I didn't bathe; my teeth were rotting in my mouth. That last night in the desert, I'm half hoping a flying saucer from Art Bell &

Company will come and take me, but I thought too, suppose my son lost me, and went through this! That would be so wrong! So I checked into a Motel 6 and slept for a week, then I drove out here."

The woman next to me was very pretty. Why hadn't I noticed or thought that before? Not just her features, but compassion that made a look of wonderment to her, and all the hard etched lines had gone from her face.

She told me about trying to get a job, trying to cover up the disorientation that swamped her, the anger she felt at being so abnormal, she called it, out of control.

"It's rough."

"Better than twice it's rough. I had some guy for some stupid job, I'm trying to get a job making smoothies in a juice bar, and he leans back and looks me up and down, and says, so, what's your story? I didn't have a story; I don't have a story, not like he meant. Creep. It was like that, all over, and I think what I worked on most was trying to disguise it so the pain wouldn't be visible and I wouldn't be asked what's my story. But you helped, really, you helped."

"Would you tell me how? I remember the things I was going through, me. I remember those three days. You slept a lot. I went to work. I was wondering all the while if you'd start doing peculiar things and get me evicted. I knew something was off in you, but it made me feel for you. We really didn't know each other. I liked you a lot, from the start, but we hardly knew each other. I was, God, Edith! I feel so selfish. I was stuck on the things going on with me. I had a lump on my breast..."

"You never told me!"

"We're a lot alike! I figured if I didn't say it out loud it would go away. I finally got it checked, nothing, a cyst, a nothing. But by then you were gone."

I got up to grab my sweatshirt and put it on. I went outside to my car to get my wool socks, good for any travelling because once the sun goes, it can drop to the forties, even mid-summer. We settled back on the couch in front of Edith's fireplace.

"You know that trail by your place?" she said. "The split, the one road following on to the ranch house, and the other one

111

goes up the hill to your place?" Edith was holding the scotch glass in her hand while she spoke, looking at the firelight through it.

"Where the macadam switches to dirt, uphill? Sure, I know it," I said, "The road to my place."

"Okay. Now I could say, with conviction, that for the better part of two years after my son's death, and then for the better part of the next three, I was really off the wall. I still don't know if it was because I couldn't talk about it, or there was no one to talk to. Everything reminded me, sounds and colors and children! Oh, God I couldn't stand to see or be near anybody under forty. I blamed myself for everything, right back to his birth."

"God, parenting is so hard, we're all ill-equipped, Edith. Not everybody takes to it like ducks to water."

"I didn't have in me what he needed from me, that's the plain truth. And maybe I do now, and maybe I don't but in either case it's too late, and that's the truth. Oh, hell, I was lost, just gone lost to it, remorse and blame and grief. Grief may be the most powerful emotion there is, and nobody would've made me believe that, before this happened. I play differently than I use to! I can hear it! Is it in my chest or hands or brain? I don't know where it resides, but it's not the same. But listen, back to those three days. Funny, you worried about me, but I've had a lot of training, maybe it's the music or what I can do with music, but it helped. I'm disciplined like nobody's business. It didn't help with my sanity, but my behavior, you know, figuring I could trust myself to not fully self-destruct."

"And coming through it, Edith, what's that journey like?"

"Well, nobody can really help. I mean, I know I said you did, and so did other people, but it's not what anyone would think, not a regular thing. It's like electric currents that finally penetrate, that get through to the brain or the heart, a little stab of insight, and then you cry and let go of some of it. The relief is what it must feel like to die."

I hadn't talked to anyone with this kind of loss before. I did feel incompetent and helpless. I had all the platitudes ready that I couldn't bring myself to say, like, he's in a better place or it was fate, or he'd finished his voyage.

Edith could see it on me, and smiled. "Don't say anything, none of it's true or logical. There's no excuse for death. I hate death. I will always loathe death. There's no way of making it pretty. It's not fair."

Edith started crying, and in a moment, she was letting it shake from inside her into waves of sobs that she made no effort to control. I sat next to her, watching the fire. After a little while, she got up and went to bed, and I went to mine. Maybe that was the help she meant. It was the first time I'd seen her cry since I met her. I figured there'd be more to say in the morning, and there was.

When I woke up, she was coming through the back door with one fist full of sunflowers and a scissors in the other. Country music was on the radio. Coffee water on the boil.

"Thanks," she said, "just sitting there and letting me let go. How'd you sleep?"

I told her it was great, the whole house was a delicious experience and asked how she managed to end up in it. Real estate was pretty high in the area. She'd left everything behind, and it had sounded like that included the bank account.

"Life is just amazing, isn't it." Edith was making a big old tin watering can ready for the sunflowers. "I told you I'd given my island to Larry and Rachel? Well, five years went by before I wrote them, I had a post office box finally. I got back this excited, wonderful letter, nine or ten pages, updating me on everything. Rachel had the second baby, they moved onto the island, Larry built some more rooms and did carpentry...he's very good...Rachel had a third baby! The second one was a girl, the third a boy, and they named him after my son. Oh the tears from that! By then life was getting complicated, she's pregnant with the fourth and they got a place on the mainland, and sold my island, with all of Larry's fine building...I'm still floored...some artist from Brooklyn bought it...get ready for this...half a million bucks! Inside the letter is a check for half! $250,000. I'm still in shock. I protested, they said I changed their lives, I deserved it and probably needed it. Am I lucky or what. New life, and money to pave the way. All of this happened two months ago."

"What good people."

113

"Yes."

❖   ❖   ❖

We went into the garden, smoked cigarettes and watched the dawn. "Look," Edith said over breakfast, which I volunteered to cook, "I need to keep getting this out of me, like putting cards on the table or something, as these things pop up out of me I don't want to hold them back anymore. I think it's death for me if I do, and maybe going crazy again, which is a dark and dreadful place I no longer want to be. There's something true about the stages, or levels of coming back to life. It never made sense to me before, I'd read that you sense it, you're stepping off one level and proceeding up to the next, and you don't even know you've been curled up in a ball, like dodging meteors, until you're in that new place and look back. Follow? Okay. Those three days at your place, it was the first rest I'd had in literally years. I was not scared. I was not in danger. I was safe. I trusted you. I slept, and I had a place to shower. It was incredibly important. I can't even say what...it was huge."

"Well, I'm glad. It seemed like so little..."

"No!" She banged her fist on the table and everything shook and the coffee sloshed through the rough pine. She dropped a napkin on it and refilled our cups.

"No, no and no. It was monumental. I want you to listen to this, because I only half believe it myself. I never said this outloud. You know something? I do have a story. This is my story. That day, the morning I left your place, listen, I'm coming from the row of garbage cans at the bottom of that hill where the paths intersect. I'd cleaned out the car and had some stuff to toss, so I walk down to the cans. Then I'm on the fork, right there where the dirt road goes up to your place, the other paved road goes off. Your place, my friend. Where I felt safe."

"Okay, I know where you mean. Edith, my friend."

"Okay, you're there?"

"Yes, I'm there." I was curious, waiting.

114

"I start back up the hill, like I said, maybe a few feet past the fork, and I look over to the main road and see a woman walking in my direction, parallel. But we're on these different roads. We're not opposite each other, maybe twenty feet apart. Me going up. I like her immediately, and don't understand. It just kind of washes over me, that this is a really terrific woman, it makes me warm. So I smile. Then, here I am on this road above the one she's on, and we're close, but not close, and it strikes me odd. But all of a sudden I stop and say to her, 'Is there anything you need?' Just that."

"Go on, go on." And I confess to a thrill sweeping me, maybe the tale itself or Edith's own excitement.

"Okay. And this hasn't taken any time at all but was one of those things where you feel slightly separated from real time, and I'm sort of puzzled but pleased, and then I start to wonder, is she really there, or am I hallucinating her. Except it's so clear. It's vivid. Sometimes when I play violin, the images from the composers are of such strength, have such powerful enormity to them, you are literally in their vision. And seeing this woman reminds me. I ask if she needs anything, meaning I suppose, from me. She looks up and smiles. She shakes her head, no. She looks down the road in front of her. And I smile back. And I'm really happy! Happy to see her! Happy she's nice! Then I get the thought, leave her alone, because she's sorting through something that's private. Well, I sure understood that! I'd been feeling that way for years, so I sure understood that!...years... so I keep on my path, and God! It keeps coming over me how good I feel! No frantic voices, no desperate pulling from twenty directions, I just feel good! I have fifty feet maybe to go on that road to your place. But I stop and turn around. I want to thank her, or wave, or something. My heart just feels so light, like it used to before, like I'm the way I used to be in life, it's so good."

"I'd have done that, follow the impulse to let her know she made me happy. You go back, talk to her?"

"No. I turn around on the hill to look at her, though. I plan to speak, there's some jumble of words in my mouth trying to match the experience. She's not there."

"She'd gone further down the road? To visit somebody?"

"No. · She's not there. She'd walked past me, gone on a different road, while I climbed up. I feel frantic for a minute, I can't stand I didn't let her know. Then I start to understand. That's when I packed up and drove away, alone, so it could sink in."

"Understand what?"

"That a big part of what I'd been going through just ended. That woman on the road, on that other path, leaving me, both of us glad we met…that was me."

VIII

Outposts, Signposts, Steamboats, and the Wild Blue Thunder on the Road to Mandalay

Outposts, Signposts, Steamboats,
and the Wild Blue Thunder on
the Road to Mandalay

I departed big city life just under a decade ago for the woods of America, and the other day in a state of reflection, I thought myself in a boat similar to the one navigated by the British civil servant to exotic ports, a century and empire past.

Rudyard Kipling and his tales of bug infested barracks, the curried acquaintanceship with custom, frenzied market places and surreal natives, long tempted me to join the fray. I now possess a kinship to his adventurers I never felt reading him, curled up on my couch in downtown Brooklyn.

I hit the road. At first like Auntie Mame with a thousand steamer trunks, then pared down, more like a travelling circus. Land somewhere and unfold the tents, open the rail cars, place the props, and I was a ready to rock'n'roll Bedouin.

Taking off was only part impulse. I no longer recognized the city I had been devoted to and loved.

❖   ❖   ❖

In the early nineties, New Yorkers were dodging machine gun fire, and tucking their children to bed in bathtubs so they wouldn't be killed by stray bullets piercing apartment walls. Homeowners and shopkeeps were hosing syringes and human excrement off sidewalks. Modern times had run amok. I'd put in 27 years on the front; I decided to head for the hills.

Winter was coming and I had finished with winter. I departed Brooklyn in search of a new life, the notes of a first novel stashed in an orange shoebox. Summer was still in the air.

I chose Virginia with the keen regional wisdom possessed by the northeasterner: Virginia was south, ergo, warm. I looked forward to frolics in the wildflowers, and swilling mint juleps in civilized company on expansive porches. It was all that, the summer I arrived at a scenic Blue Ridge Mountain outpost. I found a cedar-shingled house for rent, on three acres of trees. I could write my novel there. I painted my name on a plank, nailed it to a stake and pounded it into the soil at the edge of my driveway.

The skies were so spectacular, the night air sweet and cool, none of it familiar like the city now hundreds of miles north. I spent the first two weeks on the grass in front of my porch, stargazing till I fell asleep, waking to birds and deer and dawn and fragrant blossoms.

❖   ❖   ❖

By October the blizzards and ice storms started. By Thanksgiving the mountain was snowbound. But hellfire, it wasn't the weather that shook my innards.

Due to her own admission (and a jaunty one at that), I learned from the aging owner of my rental herself that she had been a functionary of the Third Reich, back in the good old days. It explained her fluent lapses into the tongue of the fatherland, and a certain chilling edge to her. The locals had nicknamed my landlady the nazi. It made me wonder about the neighborhood, too. Of all the things the happy realtor was proud and mandated to reveal, that was not of their number. So, I was paying monthly tribute on property owned by a nazi. Okay, there's been a lot of water under the bridge since WWII, but what was in store?

Then there was a solicitous, elderly fellow on a farm one hill over, who became first an amorous neighbor and then my own personal stalker when I rejected him. The realtor knew him, too. And more. That he'd gotten the boot, for psychiatric reasons, from a distant police force, circa 1950. When he started killing wildlife and leaving their corpses under my bedroom window, I started packing. Brooklyn has its ways, and can be dangerous, but this was a bit much. Woody paradise, where are you?

I put half my things in storage, sold a couple of pieces of furniture, and moved to a farm, hidden far far away in the civil war hills. It was a rough, crazy, icy move in the middle of the worst winter since 1750. But I was clear of the nazi. And the stalker. And his newly arrived son, a large maniacal heroin addict. Some trio.

❖   ❖   ❖

The great old farm was on seventy-five acres, had a red barn half collapsed, an old stone garden house and greenhouse, and best of all, a log cabin, something I'd wanted to live in since I was a kid and never expected to. The rent dropped by a hundred bucks.

Steady on, always looking on the bright side, I was three new chapters into the new novel and writing short stories. And so much new material! I learned how to use the log splitter, I chopped firewood, I plowed the road out, and lived on Campbell's tomato soup long enough to finally get sick of it. I wrote. In two months, the power outages were passing and the phone worked at least twice a week.

I'd forfeited my deposit from the place I'd fled. Money was short. I looked for work. I got hired to tend bar at a pretentious golf club. The owner tried one time too many to reach down my blouse, the golfers were cheap and depressed and I booked. Before I knew it, southern October III was whistling down my stovepipe. I decided to expand my horizons; go west. I sold off and gave away most of my remaining Brooklyn antiques and jewelry. It didn't amount to much, but this time, at least, I lived out the last month on my deposit.

I gathered up my six cats, faithful Brooklyn family. And the excellent, beautiful and astounding woodsman of a chocolate Labrador I'd found in the Blue Ridge hills. He was a massive dog, with an enormous head and paws, and a serious, chiseled look. I named him Rodin, after the sculptor, who had similar features and bearing. I put everything else I owned, but for my typewriter, manuscripts, blankets, food and two changes of clothes, in storage. Then bundled the living into a 1974 Suburban I bought for $500 from a local preacher. I had to coax the good reverend for three months to part with his truck, which is what he called the old Chevy. Finally, he towed it out of the turnip field from which I had longingly admired it. He and his son did a tune-up, threw in one new tire and a new battery. Having been blessed on our journey, and knowing we needed it, off we went.

The old GMC Suburban was Robin's Egg Blue, very large and very strong. Everything worked but the radio. The muffler was a much welded, uncertain thing. I named her The Blue Thunder.

My best friend in Brooklyn, Sheila, sent me a postcard of the icebound arctic boat of the hero explorer, Shackleton. I taped it to the dashboard to give me courage. I had a grandfather I hardly knew and now long gone. But he'd stowed away on an ocean freighter when he was a mere twelve-year-old, and he had red hair. That grandpa's damn the torpedoes was in me, too. There was much to push us forward. I'd had a lifetime of cold and snow, and never quite enough money to pay fuel bills through an entire winter. I'm willing to suppose Virginia had a kinder personality than the one I met, but I was glad to put all of it behind me. California sounded pretty good. We had Blue Ridge mice under the Surburban's hood, clear to Texas.

❖ ❖ ❖

We made our way south into balmy Indian summer days, over dusty secondary roads. The old truck could cruise at ninety, and held up like a champ. By Alabama, I needed three new tires, and the guy at the gas station couldn't figure out how mold and soil were packed inside the rims. I didn't tell him about the turnip field days, out of deference to The Blue Thunder's pride. She was a perfect road trip car. And we were in love. The brakes held till we hit the West Coast.

A hurricane chased us out of Galveston, but not before I got down some awesome crawfish and beer, sitting in a gray and neon dockside diner, facing the wilding-up Gulf.

123

Biloxi-Mississippi low Tide - Winter

We were ready for some time off the road. I figured Biloxi for a good regroup, but did not count on it being one of the most lavishly peculiar places on the planet. We settled into a fabulously seedy motel, which spewed character, gargantuan flying bugs, nests of fire ants in the driveway, and Spanish moss hanging like flesh off the trees. We'd made a stealthy dark of night entry, but without good cause. There is nothing, it turns out, that the night clerks of America hate so much as their jobs. They are neither inclined to peek at, nor poke at, nor deliver questions to a traveler loaded down with anything, much less cat carriers and a large dog.

Rodin and I walked the coast. The little I saw of civil war plantations and southern hero generals, the preserved bones of both, was touching. Pleasure steamboats for gamblers spiked the ten mile limit, their water wheels splashing, fairy lights against the dirty beige winter low tide. The smell of dispirit and fish, everywhere.

You have to see Biloxi to believe it. And her off-season face is the one to look for. I had a swim in the sacred eerie waters, and dodged a ticket from a dune buggy cop for having my dog on the beach. Rodin had all the adventuring of a Labrador in him, pleased to investigate every new territory. He had the habit of sitting on the edge of forest, meadow, or waterway, sizing up, and charging in, ordinances be damned.

The cats were doing wonderfully well, despite an occasional dust-up between roommates. When we made these increasingly rare motel stops, everybody came out for a good brushing and hug. The Biloxi motel bugs added an element of play and wonder. These things outdid anything I ever saw in Brooklyn.

The muffler on The Blue Thunder turned out to be a series of bumps and contortions. I hadn't thought to check until it dropped to the ground in the motel parking lot. A nice man in the room next to us volunteered to fix it with a coat hanger, and his wiring job lasted unswervingly for five years, when I finally got the whole thing replaced. I was learning that truck, and damn proud of her fortitude. Biloxi wasn't much of a rest, but it was a treat and a half, and I long to return.

Texas handed us a storm that started in my rear view mirror and was overhead an hour later, unloading such a volume of hail and rain that we had to dead stop mid highway. Five minutes later it passed by in black splendor and mile long lightning strikes, uninterrupted to New Mexico. We continued on through days of tall freeze-you're-under-arrest cactus, truck stops, and placid void.

The desert was changing. Mountains rose on the horizon. I drove through a little town so fast I had to back up to the radio store where I wanted to pick up a transistor. "How do," said the clerk, "we got'em, but you got to take it on faith." His part of Texas didn't get radio signals. Fifty miles out, the mountains in a new lineup, his guarantee proved good for the money. I was getting local weather reports crackling into The Blue Thunder, and country music to boogie down to. Hoping for the best is a way of life.

Somewhere outside Dawson, a touring couple from Germany came over to my picnic table and handed me a twenty, for the cats. At the next stop I put it to good use on a roasted chicken and a quart of cream. The Suburban got half a tank. Nice celebration. That phenomenon happened again in a ritzy coastal town. I parked in the post office lot and was off buying stamps, when some stranger opened the driver side door, ignored my large-toothed dog, and deposited a twenty-pound bag of cat kibble on the front seat. Go figure. In New York, people break into cars to take things out. God knows what we looked like. I didn't stop to worry about it, but maybe if donations happened daily, I would have. They didn't. Nor did we get arrested, or even a ticket. We sure didn't have much, and I'd left the quasi-security of roofs over our heads far behind. I wanted to make a good, spirited trip for all of us, despite the shortfalls. We were all seeing and feeling and smelling things that were entirely new. In my book, that's at least half of a good life, and I was going to secure the other half in view of the Pacific Ocean.

❖   ❖   ❖

I drove up to the California coast from San Diego, through LA's nightmare freeways you can't get on or off, sure we'd die.

The Shackleton postcard was wrapped on the steering wheel in my sweaty palm.

The plan, loosely constructed, was to head north to San Francisco. I was dreaming large. Maybe I'd start a fishing village, and we'd live on a boat. Who knew? Anything seemed possible now. I wasn't feeling reckless, but the sky was the limit.

Rodin had some particular problems with bladder control, and I figured it was from years of living his own life in the woods of Virginia, never indoors till I found him. We accommodated us both when he learned to give a stop the car woof. In the weeks of travel, it ended the problem. Not necessarily so with the rest of the world. Once indoors, it meant nightly rounds every hour or less. I had intended to stay in San Francisco and settle there, but the problems outweighed the answers, and after four days with friends, we packed up and headed south once more. Actually, and it pleased me no end, in the four days under a roof I managed to start a screenplay from one of my short stories. Maybe we'd go to Hollywood! We headed down the pitched narrow San Francisco By The Bay streets, singing California Dreamin' and On The Road Again. Feelin' the beat.

The brakes went out in Monterey. So like The Blue Thunder not to produce emergencies; we were on a flat road going 5 mph. However, it was six pm on a Saturday night, in a strange town. The transmission had been leaking since Davenport. We crept into a handy RV parking lot off Cannery Row. I took Rodin for a walk on the bicycle path, wondered what Steinbeck would have done, happily remembered the Joad family's overloaded truck, and tucked us all in for the night.

Early Sunday morning at a slow and breathless creep, I spotted an open garage in Seaside, and we glided in. The mechanic was suffering from a ferocious migraine, being tailed by a tan spiritualist with vibrating copper rods and magnets to rid him of it, but he managed to fix my brakes and did something intelligent with the transmission. For six hours, my cats and dog and manuscripts were suspended on a lift while I drained the ATM, and called some friends back east to float me a loan. It was a grim day, most of the future rent and deposit money on an apartment going to repair the apartment we were most likely to be staying in,

127

The Blue Thunder Dew Drop Inn. But there were still places I wanted to see, and I was managing to write several hours a day. Small bits of cleverness made the truck highly livable. Maybe we'd have a life on the road some more. I was proud of all of us staying together, and the loss of comfort I could have had alone wasn't worth worrying about.

We kept going further south on Coastal Highway One, to Pfeiffer State Park in Big Sur. Now there's a place that has always meant untold freedom and raw natural beauty to me, and I used to dream of at least seeing it, way back in Brooklyn, New York, with seven million neighbors. For fifteen dollars a night and one dollar more for the dog, we got a campsite and I rigged up a tent. Somehow, in the miracle ways of the universe, I met the camp hosts, David and Nancy, the day before Thanksgiving. Rodin and I got an invite to dinner. I doubt I'll ever know a sweeter, more interesting pair. Nancy was a biologist and David an inventor. My spirits soared with the contact, and they fed us a fantastic trailer-kitchen-produced Thanksgiving dinner: turkey, cranberry sauce, mashed potatoes, the works. David built a huge campfire in the pit next to their trailer canopy, hot enough to fight the day's drizzle. I left with a baggie of leftovers for the cats (they had four of their own), and full of stories finely told over pumpkin pie, red wine, and the glow of life. Solace when you're braced for anything but, comes from strangers. And I made friends forever.

By now, the big rains of '96 had started, and didn't stop until they flooded the entire central coast. I worked on my novel until we were forced to evacuate by rangers. David and Nancy got relocated to a safer spot. Helicopters were rescuing tourists and dropping supplies to mountain houses. Less than half a mile away, Highway One was collapsing under walloping mudslides and wind. Bixby Bridge was on the skids. I taped Shackleton's boat to the dashboard. Half the campsites in the park were under water. We were given the option to move to higher land. I wrote another chapter with a flashlight taped to an old felt hat.

For more than a week, the rain subsided to a sprinkle. The sun came out. Light filtered through massive prehistoric redwoods, taller than the eye could calculate, wider than four people hand to hand could span. A floorbed of ferns raised up to

the sun against the orange trunks, pushing their way through pine needles and cones, and fallen branches. I tidied up the campsite, repacked the car, and washed out clothes in the camp laundry sink that never dried. I wasn't a high maintenance chick, but I liked a good shampoo. More than once I blessed the camp's concrete and pine showers, where you got plenty of hot water for your two bits.

One dry day at my picnic table, the sun sizzling through the wet wood, we got a visit from a young forlorn wanderer. He had a sorry looking dog on a rope, and an overloaded backpack weighing him down. I never got too deep into his troubles, but I laid out a spread and invited him to sup. I think he was a runaway, and maybe sixteen. I had gotten a red and white checked plastic tablecloth and put it out for the feast. I had herring in sour cream, some great bread and cheese, Campbell's tomato soup bubbling in a pot on the fire we built, a bottle of Jack Daniel's, and some borderline chocolate cake. Despite the riches, he was a sorrowful kid. Whatever he needed, and it was much, I could only offer a free meal. I had my hands full and survival was touch and go. I didn't hold out hope for him, but I wished him all the luck in the world when I finally asked him to go, as he was seriously bringing us all down. Rodin cheered up his dog, and I gave him two more cans of food beyond the two the poor thing had gulped down.

❖   ❖   ❖

Around this time, I got to talking to a ranger I kept running into. He taught me a Buddhist chant to improve prosperity, and hired me on for a long weekend of digging trenches alongside his new house in some obscure town I can't remember, fifty miles inland and north. He also sprang for lunch each day. The town was toward a desert, and the sun was out. Damn good three days. Of course, wherever I went, my darlings were at my side.

The '74 Suburban's roomy second row of seats was lodging for my Labrador. I had stuffed things in front of the seats and covered it all with quilted moving blankets, down comforters and pillows, the way my family had done for the kids on lengthy vacations. The huge two-cat-per carriers had blankets, kitty pans,

130

dry and wet food in separate bowls, and water. When we stopped, I'd roll up the windows to an inch, and they'd all come out for a stretch and romp.

Three out of the six cats could be trusted not to climb trees or run off and terrify me, and they had the redwood experience first hand. For the others, I brought pinecones inside. It was stimulating for us all. And I alternated their views by addressing their carriers to various directions. If it looked like somebody was missing somebody else, I'd switch roommates.

Two of the cats, Noel and Nod One Night, got good at riding shotgun without heading for the floor pedals. In all, they were excellent troopers, brave to a cat. If I thought we were in danger of being stopped or inspected, I covered the lot with a sheet and boxes. I had jackets hanging on the back rafters of the endlessly long truck, and we stayed clear of trouble. My entourage, feline and canine made it impossible (with a few disastrous exceptions) to find a place to rent, so I didn't. I don't know what's going on with America, and maybe it's the wildly exaggerated real estate values of our times. But having even one animal has turned into a liability, and it's shameful.

❖   ❖   ❖

Before Christmas, the rains had returned full force and relentless. I volunteered for sandbagging at the riverbanks, and lowest parts of the highway. But I could see the handwriting on the wall, and we made a run for food the second or third day in, along the slim steep road of what was left of Coastal Highway One. Boulders bounced across the torn and split asphalt, blew off the cliffs, and leapt into the Pacific below. We got to the Safeway in Carmel, couldn't get back onto the road and spent three days in the parking lot until a sheriff, gun drawn, tapped on my midnight window and told me to vamoose by sunup. "Where?" I remember asking him sleepily. "You can't stay here," he said, and indeed, the parking lot had flooded overnight.

By late morning we'd sloshed back to the highway and were told it was cleared for traffic, with no guarantees. We drove

down past Big Sur this time, some thirty miles to Julia Pfeiffer State Park, famous for its two hundred-foot waterfall out of the forest, into the ocean.

Once inside this smaller Pfeiffer Park, we risked forbidden overnighters. Fortunately, there was so much chaos elsewhere, nobody noticed us for two weeks. I met my pals David and Nancy again, who were being evacuated to Andrew Molera Park, north by fifty miles, to drier land. They warned me of the hazards. My options were sorely limited. David pointed out a few good spots, Nancy drove their camper under a secreted stand of sturdy trees for us to live in, off the ground and dry. I decided to risk it. There was some propane left in the heater's tank. I sure didn't have to worry about water. We parted.

Frankly, it was like moving into the Ritz. I could stand up and walk around; the cats were free and cozied into corners. Rodin had no use for rain and limited his excursions out. And I'd found a dry overhang, where, sheltered by a large umbrelled branch I could stoke a grill and cook pancakes. Is anything cheerier than a pancake? Inside, everything I owned smelled of warmed up wet dog.

❖   ❖   ❖

It was pretty stunning. The waterfall, on the other side of the highway, was wildly violent. The river had swollen to landmark levels. Cliffs were emulsified and sliding trees toppled and crashed, some awfully close by. I kissed the Shackleton boat, and wrote by kerosene light and wondered more than once if there wasn't an easier way to write a novel. We were low on everything but hope. We polished off the last of the bear claws, canned and dry food, and powdered milk. I wrote letters that would be weeks late in mailing.

❖   ❖   ❖

133

By February, the landscape was drying out. Nonetheless, the outdoor thing was losing some of its original charm. I was having dreams about indoor plumbing. Which led us to a room to let in Seaside, just north of Monterey, site of the major brake repair that had changed our destiny. The room was in the middle of a home where a divorcing couple was playing out a high drama. The wife's housekeeping left much to be desired. Rodin had a yard share with her two unpleasant, biting dogs, and didn't want to stay. The cats could live in my room in their carriers. The landlady was on heavy sedatives, but I remain unconvinced she'd have been different off them. She was greedy, empty, and prying. We lasted a month. She still owes me the deposit. And one of her dogs bit off the end of Noel's tail as he swept in under the hall door. Blood everywhere, but no damage after the screaming stopped, at least that my poor Noel could communicate to me.

The landlady was the one who belonged in a carrier. And for sure, she was not the first greedy Californian I'd run into, and not the last with a touch of lunacy under the tan patina. But I'd written another chapter in Seaside, sitting on a mattress and box spring and clean sheets, under a bulb powered by electricity, and a shower and toilet in the room next door.

We went back to Big Sur, and got the same, now dried out and leafy, campsite. Rodin and I both felt liberated. The cats stopped excessive shedding that the hounds of Seaside had inspired. It may not have been fabulous back in the woods, but it was divine. I lived on unheated food, like sardine sandwiches spread thick with mayo, salt, pepper and garlic. We all shared roasted chickens. I drank bottled coffee, bottled juices, bottled water, and with no rent to pay, ate like royalty. But we'd gone through a costly month. The veterinarian bills for Noel's tail for one thing. And Rodin was off his feed a little, and I couldn't seem to make him fully happy or comfortable. That vet cost $150, to proffer the opinion that nothing was wrong.

The rains had pretty much done their damage and gone. Volunteer sandbagging was underway and road crews everywhere. The landscape burned orange with slickers, vests, and traffic cones. Along with it, the job market was opening up as life returned to the peninsula. I got hired at a bronze foundry and learned wax chasing

and patina. The wages were minimum and the conditions medieval. Six months later we came to a parting. I'd had three of my own bronzes cast. I kept writing.

❖   ❖   ❖

The chance for four weeks of house painting on a millionaire's house in Carmel came my way. The contractor took me out for martinis every night after work at Clint Eastwood's Hog's Breath Inn. I ran the length of Carmel Beach with Rodin at sunset and dawn.

Mostly we kept living in the state parks in Big Sur. I was on the yearlong waiting list at the post office and getting mail in General Delivery. Around July, short of funds and hearing a lot of talk about some place called Carmel Valley, I packed up and out we went, about fifteen miles inland from the ocean.

I got a waitress job in a cute little restaurant, rented a room from the couple who ran it and owned the house in the back, and built an outdoor shelter for my cats. Rodin had a place to romp with their big yellow lab, and strolls in the nearby park. It had been about nine months since we'd left Virginia. This was the first time I thought maybe just, we'd settle down and I could earn enough to get a bigger place. Carmel Valley was really beautiful. Soft rolling hills that went to a sueded tan from winter green, mists that hovered their tops and crevices, and flowers of the oddest shapes and strongest purples, oranges, and yellows. The sun was out and hot year round, and if the nights were in the 40's, midday was near 90 degrees. It was a place I'd be happy in.

I had a long interview to get the waitress job, including proof of citizenship from many documents and a thumb print on file. Anyway, I should have interviewed the boss (also owner, and chef). He turned out to be a former gangster from back east with a propensity for provoking assaults. I hate to tell you how that little tidbit came to light. For reasons known only to God, on our busiest Sunday brunch, the chef/owner started slamming omelets he didn't like the look of onto the kitchen walls. Customers were waiting, the mood was frantic. Without so much as a howdedo, the

136

gangster gourmet came at me fast with a 12-inch kitchen knife. He ended up in jail. The DA concurred that I was innocent.

If Brooklyn had ever been as wild as California, I wasn't remembering it that way. But the case against him was strong, and the 911 call came from his wife, screaming bloody murder into a tape recorder. Between tears as he was carted off, I swore to help her keep the place running and she swore she'd get a divorce. We both got orders of protection the next day. Three days later, returning with groceries, I opened the back door to the kitchen, and there he was! Standing at the stove, cooking! He slowly turned around, put his fingers to his lips, and said, "shhhhhh…" like something out of Fellini married to Hitchcock. I peed in my pants on the run to my car. No, his wife wasn't buried under fresh concrete. She'd bailed him out, and was standing by him, both of them now against me. It didn't last, of course. By the time she came to her senses he was sentenced to five months in the hoosegow.

At least I'd earned a lot of money, which took some of the edge off being suddenly homeless and jobless and scared witless. Somehow I'd managed to write three new chapters on my novel between shifts. I taped Shackleton's ship to my breast, and drove down to Pfeiffer.

We took a week to calm down. When I called one of the women I'd waitressed with, she told me about a place in Carmel Valley I could rent, and keep the animals. It was a horse ranch, further out than I'd explored, and they had bunkhouses to let. One had just opened up. I drove out and applied. It was a nine by twelve foot room with one window, sink and toilet, and cheap. I took it. The cats and I slept on the floor on a bedroll, and found a scorpion under the pillow one night which I ushered outside, fascinated, none of us the worse for the wear.

❖   ❖   ❖

Rodin was very sick. He was in intensive care in the local animal hospital, connected to tubes and nearly unable to stand. I was looking for work, but my heart and soul were attached to the hospital. I couldn't think straight. I missed him more than I could stand. I was allowed to see him twice a day. He had kidney failure, and the doctor thought it was probably congenital. He would be allowed to live at the bunkhouse when he came home. That was enough to keep me going.

The bunkhouses were attached seven in a row. I could hear the woman next door flossing her teeth, and the guy on the other side swallowing beer and playing with his radio. So I did a lot of hiking. I was trying to sort out all we'd been through, and the brand new sorrow of maybe losing my precious dog. Why was it so damn hard to get a foothold again? I was working, even if the pay was bad. I was writing with great regularity, my eye on a better future. I sure didn't expect any of us to be sacrificed along the way, but the way had been long and rough. Rodin wouldn't have lasted outdoors one more Virginia winter. I was convinced of that. And I made every accommodation for the animals on the road, because I loved them. The month before, I'd gotten news that two close friends of mine had died back east. I was experiencing a lot of loss, and wasn't so sure I was going to make it.

People who do their own work, like writing or art, tend to be constantly pumping up their hope. You even gather what you can from the darkest days, sure that better days are coming. Sometimes, even hope gives out.

After four weeks in intensive care, and with a brief rally, my beautiful, splendid Labrador, Rodin, died. I buried him, nearly paralyzed with grief, in Big Sur, in a magnificent place with a grand panorama of the ocean, the greatest span of water he'd ever met, loved, and conquered. Pine trees, Scottish Broom, and wildflowers now surrounded the best friend I'd ever had.

❖   ❖   ❖

My six cats had survived. There were trips to the vet to check this and that, but they were in pretty good shape, despite an average age of twelve years or more. I had a $2,500 bill to pay

Rodin's doctor, but they'd taken care of Rodin, on faith, not cash, and I wanted to keep my side of the bargain.

I got another waitress job, this time in a happy madhouse in Carmel that served locals, run by a surfer and his heavily accented Dutch father. My days were filled with lively chat, bronzed athletes, and the best pancakes, Eggs Benedict, and homemade bread west of New York City. I came back to the bunkhouse at night, always thinking I'd see Rodin, and I still do, wherever I am. How I miss throwing my arms around him.

The restaurant job lasted about a year. Despite the good times, the owner fired me. He said I didn't have a clue about waitressing. I was a bit distracted, and I admit it. More than that, I was less and less cut out to work for other people anymore. It grated on me that in California you "enter the service industry." How appalling. In New York, waitressing is until the Broadway gig comes through. The great outdoors remained the lure for me. I wouldn't move to a city again. And I wanted to keep writing. It would stabilize our futures.

I'd had some serious careers back east, but you wed yourself fulltime to a real job like that. I wanted to have the freedom to do relatively mindless work that only demanded a huge tolerance of arrogance from customers, who'd tip for the trouble. So I kept looking and applying and writing.

During my unemployment, I took odd painting jobs, like picnic tables at the local pizzeria, and old restored British telephone booths. Then I got hired to help manage weddings at the ranch where I was living. No commute expenses, lots of free food, and enough to cover rent.

❖   ❖   ❖

The horses on the ranch were fabulous, and I made friends with many of them. My neighbor across the way had a great Jack Russell terrier. He was no Rodin, but a lot of fun to play with. One morning at dawn I found a young opossum outside my door. He looked bewildered then scared, then dropped with a thud. They really do play dead. I picked it up and kept it in a cat carrier in the bathroom, and for two weeks fed it cat food and cream, both of which it loved. It doubled in size. For some reason, my exuberant reports on his progress alarmed the front office. When I finally agreed to release the opossum one night, he just sat there, not moving, staring at his surrogate mother, and I had to force myself away. By morning, he had taken off, hopefully to join his kind.

I had been eyeing a barn on the ranch's hilltop, used to corral tractors and feed. It had a tack room running alongside the cavernous structure. I rented the tack room and turned it into a studio. It was five times the size of the bunkhouse. There was no toilet, no shower, no hot water, and no kitchen. By the end of two months I'd added all that, and my efforts tripled my rent. And I had to provide my own heat. A little kerosene heater that looked like R2D2 did the trick. Nonetheless, it was quiet, private and at least six hundred square feet. I was glad to have it.

Most landlords in California would be arrested in New York City for what they call rentals and collect money. On the Monterey Peninsula, a kitchen is a rare luxury. If there's a bathroom at all, you use that sink for dishes (and sometimes bathing), and a hotplate or electric wok to cook. But the weather's glorious, the scenery spectacular, and (with the exception of the year I arrived), you can spend eleven and a half months out of the twelve in both. The ranch had a swimming pool, and I was the only one who ever used it. It was nestled in a mountainside, overflown by eagles and condors and hawks. I got a tan. Like so many other things in life, there was a tradeoff.

The ranch sheep and goats ate my lavender bushes down to stubs, then played catch with the root balls. You couldn't tell them a thing. Along with two donkeys and a mule, they did what they chose and were perfectly charming at it. The lot were corralled next to me. If they got to butting heads in the stalls at the far side of my bathroom, everything crashed off my walls.

The barn's tractors roared to attention at six am and shook the tack room. But because they carried the sweet smelling alfalfa to the marvelous pastured horses, it was easy to forgive, and I'm an early riser. At a more sociable morning hour, the horsey women arrived, screeching and currying. They were unforgivable. All of them parked their Porsches and Jaguars and their boarded thoroughbreds outside my door.

❖   ❖   ❖

My novel was wonderful, but a mish-mosh of disconnected characters, and the story line was going south. Too much electrifying stimulus in its formation. However, I was pleased that I'd begun to teach myself to write a novel. So, I set the first one aside, and wrote a love story about a Louisiana wildcatter I'd met in Coney Island twenty years ago, instead. I finished it, all 357 pages, and called it NOISE. I started looking for an agent.

The response was swift and enthusiastic. I got me a NYC agent in a month, and he signed me to a two-year contract for all rights, starting August 2001. Ride 'em cowgirl! But, three weeks later, 911 happened to my old hometown, and Pennsylvania, and Washington, D.C., and my beloved America.

My agent, his company, and family were okay. A year went by. Inexplicably, the man never sent out a word of my novel and the words he'd been so crazy about to a single publisher. He made 'contacts'. I only know that much by calling his office after ten months of not hearing from him. Then he complained I was the type that needed too much pampering!! I fired him. Breach of contract. I was furious at the wasted time, and the unworkable system of publishing.

Meanwhile, back at the ranch, the horsey activity in front of my door had reached a feverish pitch. My barn had turned into a trendy spot for lessons, visits, grooming, cell phones, trucks, trailers, and rock'n'roll.

I set to focusing on NOISE (the novel) again, and sent out inquires to agents who'd been keen the year before. I kept my p.o. box in Carmel Valley. I packed up. Two years before, I'd had everything moved out from storage in Virginia. I had a household again, at least in moveable bulk, the remains of what I held dear.

141

I rented a seventeen-foot U-Haul in Monterey, and my friend Debi and her son, Zac, drove that, her pick-up on a trailer towed behind them. She was always up for an adventure.

We headed the caravan, The Blue Thunder in the lead, up to the Sierra Nevadas, a hundred and fifty miles northeast. Rodin would have thought it swell. They'd all have thought it swell.

Four of my cats, whom I loved with all my heart, protected, and wept over, died in those previous years, of untold things or old age. I buried them on the ranch. Nod One Night, 8; Isabel, 22; Angel Wings, 14; Noel, 19. My precious calico, Astrid, had been poisoned. Only Gorgeous remained, a robust, all white, twelve-year-old Brooklyn born boy with one green eye and one blue, son of Babette and Clarence. (He couldn't hear, all his teeth were gone, and his right ear was slightly cauliflowered from a fight in his youth, but I wasn't past confessing to some wear myself.) We were eight years out of New York and five from Virginia. What would this mountain range hold for us? I had no idea.

I opened the local newspaper at a breakfast diner overlooking Bass Lake in Yosemite, and stared at a state park flyer, which exclaimed in thick black ink: WARNING! YOU ARE ENTERING ACTIVE BEAR COUNTRY! Next to it an ink drawing of a demo bear, fangs a-sparkle. The Shackleton postcard was still with me, taped to The Blue Thunder's visor.

After another half an hour of driving, we disembarked at a small cabin I'd found for rent in the woods. My friend, Rhiannon, and her husband, met us there and we all got the truck unloaded and my things set up inside. Debi and Zac would stay overnight. Rhiannon had thoughtfully brought us dinner, and we had a great rousing, exhausting welcome home party. I liked everything about it. We were at about six thousand feet altitude, near Fish Camp and fifteen minutes form the great Yosemite Sequoia groves. I found the sign I'd made with my name on it and first planted in Virginia. It was somewhat weathered. I put it at the end of a flowerbed. Gorgeous was crazy about all the windows and birds.

❖   ❖   ❖

For the first two weeks, everything was fine. There's something about that time frame and human reaction, and if wrong is where you're headed, it blooms in 14 days. The property owner was an old hippie with a mountain man's waist-length white beard, and as it turned out, had a fondness for gin, morphine and LSD. His mood swings were a wild ride.

I'd been trying to organize my first novel and all the parts I liked. But my new home in the wilderness surrounded by pioneer and goldminer history, mountain lions, bears, and a lunatic landlord on opiates, proved untenable. The human interruptions were rattling, not, after all, the wildlife. Well-digging, construction on my roof and porch were never ending, and always an emergency! Emergency! Emergency! He walked in whenever he chose. I battled for my privacy to no effect. I got very depressed. After four months of invading work crews interspersed with days of eerie silence, and being unable to work, I bit the bullet and we moved again. I still haven't gotten my deposit returned, but hope springs eternal.

❖   ❖   ❖

I'm writing this from another cabin in the Sierra Nevadas. The Blue Thunder is parked on a gravel road fifty feet away, and now painted to look like a woody, and sporting many new parts since it's turnip field home of long ago.

Gorgeous sits glued to the front windows to watch the quail, antennae quivering, ten to fifteen at a time, and their military filing and pecking at the birdseed we put out. My cat has four favorite inside places with varying light and heat or cool breezes, and pillows. He's all response, either talk or purr. A writer's cat.

Digger and Ponderosa pine line a pond down the hill, thirty feet from my back porch. The oaks and aspen are very old. Fallen orange needles hush the ground and decorate massive granite boulders, and yet the sun finds its way through it all and bathes it gold. The pond colors give the air an unearthly lavender that is stunning.

Old fruit trees, apple and pear, and almond trees, planted ages ago, line the ponds and roads, and are due for a bloom. The sun has been out all winter and now it's rarely below sixty degrees. When clouds appear, they are miles wide and high, skirting the Sierra Nevada's snow white tops, an Ansel Adams photograph no matter which way you turn. So far, there are two mallard ducks and one white heron on my pond, and bullfrogs of impressive size. I plan to get a rowboat

This landowner, this time, is about eighty-five years old, and cleanshaven, and of rugged European stock. He has an interesting character. Quite a lot of it. And a touch of John Muir the botanist in him. He shares his forty acres with his three dogs, Peaches, Frisky, and Goldie, a family of Rottweilers mixed with something. He owns a piece of land about five miles toward town, and just last year finished building a two thousand square foot house on it. Once upon a time, he crossed Alaska on horseback. Now I'm living here. God help us all, I hope it lasts. He did ask for a deposit, but I'm hedging.

I've been moved in for ten days now. Four days ago, a neighbor accused Peaches and Goldie of biting his puppy. There have been ongoing trespassings, and warring tribes and uprisings at my pond, I now learn. Along with illicit beer drinking and some bad blood. Ah, wilderness. Thursday, Animal Control left a note on our gate, demanding that Peaches and Goldie be surrendered and destroyed. It's Monday and nobody's slept for four days. Fences and kennels are being repaired and installed.

I got on the phone to the sheriff, and said something was fishy: no proof or investigation. I demanded a standby, both the law and an ambulance. I started calls at six am, and the list includes the local newspaper, a friendly gallery owner down the road, the Animal Control Director, the District Attorney, and the landlord's doctor who's been treating him for heart attacks, two in the last year. We're going to keep him and the dogs alive.

My splendid IBM Selectric II is in crisis. The closest repairman is back in Monterey. The keys lock, and it doesn't do upper case, or "s" or double u. But damned if I haven't got five good chapters put together, building to an emerging plot. I've slipped Biloxi in, and am leaning toward a murder mystery which I may have a knack for, and added a couple of knuckleheads on drugs.

I think I spotted a rowboat on the pond yesterday under a lot of brush. When we get the dog thing resolved, and we will, I'll see if it floats. I need to build my water skills for the outriggers of Fiji.

I've decided to save up and publish my own writing, with a firm located in Canada. Spring is on the way. I figure to finish the first novel afloat on my pond. I'll publish them both in summer; novel one, called WHIRLPOOL, and the second one I finished first, NOISE.

Look for major feature films to follow. I can't help it. It's California. And the dawn comes up like thunder.

The Blue Thunder

THE GANDY DANCER
&
Other Short Stories

BIOGRAPHY

BARBARA D. SPARHAWK is an unusual woman who has been: the only outdoor female scaffold-climbing billboard painter in the USA; a radio producer; congressional press secretary; writer for CBS, ABC & FOX TV news, & The New York Post. She's had her own sign painting, portrait, and mural businesses; plaster and paint contractor; wax-chaser in a bronze foundry; sculptor, and more. And says she would still choose scary-thrilling entrepreneurial razzamadazz above all else.

SPARHAWK was commissioned for original oil portraits of William F. Buckley, Jr.; and James M. Fox (former head of the NY FBI), completed from sittings. Her work is in wide-ranging private collections.

She designed and sculpted models for a commissioned heroic-sized bronze memorial to slain police officers of NYC (The Officer and the Angel). Her artwork has appeared in major motion pictures, animated films, and commercials. She was a photographer's assistant for tv's SURVIVOR-AFRICA, 2001 (CBS).

B.D. SPARHAWK lives in Big Sur with her cat, Gorgeous, and the Blue Thunder. She has been driven her whole life by curiosity and the chance to witness.

She is currently working on her second novel, WHIRLPOOL, and new children's books. Her first novel, NOISE, will be published soon.

ADDITIONAL BOOKS
by
B.D. Sparhawk

Children's Book
COCO NO (Trafford Publishing 2003)

Soon to be Published

Novels
NOISE
THE WHIRLPOOL
BLUEMONT JOURNAL
SHOOT THE MESSENGER

Children's Books
THE TWO-PILLOW CAT
WHAT DOES IT MEAN TO BE GOOD
THE ONE AND ONLY ORIGINAL DOCTOR
   MANXI AND HER INIMITABLE BEAR (series)
QUESTRAL
THE MAN WHO SPOKE IN FLOWERS
THE REMARKABLE LIFE OF GINGER SNAP